Dr. Shauntey James

MURDER

Secrets Among Colleagues

Publishing Services provided by Paper Raven Books LLC

Printed in the United States of America

First Printing, 2022

Murder is *one* option!!.

Thank you for everything!!.

Blessings always

PJames

Dedication

Thank you to the Paper Raven family for ensuring that the book was done in a timely manner and carrying me through the publication process.

To Uncle Crump, Tia, and Arnetra, thank you for creating a space in which I know that I am loved and capable of doing anything that I desire. I can only hope and pray that I give this same gift to each of you.

To my nephew Martel, thank you for providing me with so much joy as I watch the next generation of our family grow. I will always love you.

To Marlene, our journey together has included so many wonderful and eventful moments and memories. I could not have done this project without you. In many ways, the book is a testament to the life that you ensured would have everything. I can never repay you for all that you have done for me. I can only say that you have made me into the person that you see today. A person who is aware of her space, her shine, and what she has to offer to society. Love always.

Last but not least, thank you to my heavenly father! This has been an interesting ride!

Chapter One
Dr. Joanna Taylor

MONDAY NIGHT

For this meeting to have any hope of running smoothly, I needed to get everything perfect in how I arranged the room. If the wrong people sat next to each other, all hell could break loose, so I arrived at the Mill Run University library early. We all needed this national grant to catapult our academic careers in various directions. This grant would yield numerous publications for years and other lucrative opportunities. I would finally be able to get my chair off my back, and the publications would aid in my tenure review package. My chair really did not like the way I looked even though I had the highest Student Rating of Teaching Effectiveness (SRTEs) campus-wide and two publications within my first term of this year. I also wanted to set up everything so Dr. Sarah Petrot (Rot) would not be upset. I needed her to stay on this project. I had worked with her since graduate school, and I knew that her contribution would be priceless. She would keep us on track, and everything would be done ahead of schedule, but I knew that she would not be happy about the membership of the group. The group included Dr. Bronston Everstone (Bron), Dr. Alfred Brown, and Dr. Pricilla Appleton.

The first person to arrive was Bron. "Did Rot get into the building yet?"

"No."

"You know she is never going to go for this?" expressed Bron.

"I will convince her that it is in our best interest to do this, and her past research will aid in getting the application process done quickly. She loves a situation in which she can maximize her work effort."

"The Title IX hearing filed by Marie Walker starts and will hopefully end tomorrow. Rot is finishing a presentation in her graduate class right now concerning sexual misconduct. Hence my question of whether she reached the building yet, or did she find out that I am on this team and walk back to her office? She has no problem telling people that she is done, and there is no need to talk to her, signaling the end of her interaction with you," articulated Bron.

This was just Rot's way. She ignored people once she was done with them, but she was never rude. She would just make the choice to not acknowledge you in the hallway or any other situation. If the situation demanded an interaction, she would be cordial, but that was it. In her mind, there was no need to have an exchange. You would think that this would not bother anyone, but most people hated it. It was like she was saying nonverbally that you were not worth her breath or, in some circumstances, that you were lower than trash.

"Your hearing will be done tomorrow, Bron. Rot cannot make a legal argument concerning your membership. We must battle her with facts. You will win your case, so she cannot bring it up. She respects people who can back up their statements."

"I know, but she can be a bear when she has determined that she is right. It is like being back in graduate school. You know you are either on her team or off," replied Bron.

"I know."

"She has no middle ground. She is particular about the people she decides to include within her work life. She keeps that group small, and each person serves a purpose," indicated Bron.

"I know."

"She is not going to make an exception and work with me. I hate that I need her, but she is on fire within the criminal justice field. She has so many publications this year alone. Two books in one year. She does not sleep. Her name will carry weight with the project. But Rot is working with Ms. Walker, Marie's mother," stated Bron.

"This aspect has not been confirmed."

"So, I guess we are going to ignore this aspect, especially tonight. You know she gives at least six presentations per year concerning women's rights," declared Bron.

"The focus tonight is on this grant and opportunities for the future. Do not underestimate that she is a businesswoman."

"I never underestimate her. She has cloaked her involvement by providing specific knowledge in her classroom and by providing educational experiences, such as guest speakers, for the entire campus. How quaint of her to use the university policy," remarked Bron.

"What? When did you find this out?"

"I found out about her involvement at the top of last week. Rot is giving my legal team a run for their money. She has been introducing university policy, which my legal team is unfamiliar with," said Bron.

"Really?"

"Yes, the team is unfamiliar with the specific details. I have a team of lawyers, and Marie has only one woman. How is one person able to keep up with a team?" asserted Bron.

"How?"

"I will tell you. Rot. I also assume that she is calling in some favors. You know she still has friends in the legal world in two states," stated Bron.

"I know."

"We argued about her involvement all last week. I told her she is overstepping her position on campus or that her position could be in jeopardy because she is getting involved in my situation," said Bron.

"You have been arguing with her for the past few months."

"I argue with Rot at least three times a month about various aspects. For example, how I treat my students. She needs to mind her business. Each student on my team has at least one publication or more in most cases. She told me that my inappropriate behavior is a reflection on the entire department," pronounced Bron.

"Really?"

"Yes. She took this same argument point (my behavior) to our boss, Dr. Melvin Peaboy. I am sorry—she 'discussed' (her words) this point with him. He did not want to discuss that point, but he *did* want to remind her to remove herself from anything associated with *my* situation. She of course, told him that he could not micromanage her classroom content or reduce her ability to provide educational experiences for the entire campus," articulated Bron.

"She is fearless. Did you doubt that she would have a response for your chair?"

"No. But he does not like *confrontation* of any kind (like your boss). On top of everything, the media picked up the case. I wonder who put that in place—Rot, the student, or her family?" uttered Bron.

"What?"

"Yes, there will be media here tomorrow. My legal team confirmed it this morning," declared Bron.

"What are you going to do?"

"Do what I always do: smile and keep it moving," answered Bron.

"Why does your chair engage her?" I needed to change the topic.

"He is trying to prove to the department that he has control, especially of her. Each time he engages with her, he loses respect in the department. She wins every argument because she backs up her point," pronounced Bron.

"He still does not realize this aspect. It is like climbing up a steep hill that he will never master. She has gone to school to debate people. She has honed this skill."

"It is a running joke behind his back. These haters have made my life a living hell. Ms. Walker is poised to begin protests starting tomorrow. Can you believe that? My name is being plastered around campus," cried Bron.

"How did you find that out about the protest? Did they get a permit?" I knew from working with Rot that most universities required a permit to protest, or the university could easily shut down an event quickly.

"You know my fraternity brothers and I know most of the information on campus," said Bron.

"Most?"

"Maybe all. It is helpful to have an active chapter on campus. I know a lot of things before they happen. My fraternity brothers warned me to never meet female students alone. I should have taken their advice," Bron affirmed, smirking.

"Once this is over, you can put this all behind you. Rot will also have to put it behind you. She follows the rule."

"But she always finds a loophole. Who would have thought she would find a loophole so quickly concerning graduate students returning after receiving a bad grade in a *single* class?" Bron enunciated.

"I did, and so did you."

"I know. I just wanted to add a dramatic flair to the question. I swear she looked at that policy for only two days, went to a few lower-level meetings before getting invited to the Faculty Senate, and forced everyone to bend her way, which they did," pronounced Bron.

"She lost a lot of friends that day on the faculty board and obtained a stalker."

"Did she really obtain a stalker or another person that hates her?" questioned Bron.

"The student is stalking her."

"Look, she is a determined person once she decides on something. It is going to be done. Did you really doubt she was going to win in record time?" stated Bron.

"No."

"Exactly," said Bron.

Relationships could be very murky on a college campus. The rumor which I let circulate was that Rot worked with me in order to ensure that I got my job at Mill Run, but I also got help from a friend. I was not in her department but in the sociology department. She helped me put my package together, and we practiced several days before the interview. She did not take anything for granted, and she wanted me to be ready for any questions. On the last day of preparation, I presented in front of a few students and faculty. She called in some favors, but I got the feeling that the individuals in the room would help her regardless. Most of the students, I found out later, she had either helped get a job, an internship, or a publication in an undergraduate journal.

A publication in an undergraduate journal was rare; thus, she placed these students on the fast track to graduate school. I knew she also had a connection to most of the faculty in the room. She had either helped them with a research project or got them a paying public speaking gig.

She was not loved by all, but the students, staff, and faculty that loved her were loyal and would move heaven and earth to help her. In some cases, I thought some people would kill for her. She was strategic in everything that she did. You thought you understood her plan, but she had already taken five steps beyond your one. You were just a piece on *HER* board of life. Rot's determination and drive was what we needed on the team, but we also needed Bron. I knew Bron's name carried a huge amount of weight on the national academic stage before his situation. He had obtained several state and national grants, some by name recognition alone.

Last week, I confirmed that President Becky Miller would write a support letter to help the team even though Marie had filed a complaint against Bron. The conversation was awkward, but businesslike. I felt like Rot was in the room for some reason. I knew that once we secured the grant, the university would be elevated on several levels, so I understood why President Miller was willing to help ensure that we completed the application process. She pointed out that Dr. Petrot needed to be a part of the team to seal the deal because the optics of her presence would cover Dr. Everstone's digressions. Her behavior signaled to me that she was not sure that the complaint would result in the removal of Bron or, at least, she was hedging her bets.

Marie was Bron's graduate teaching assistant (TA), who accused him of sexual assault. This might be the wrong term. Rot would be furious with me if she heard me using the wrong term. She was a stickler about terms. It was sexual misconduct on a college campus and not sexual assault. Regardless, I was having a hard time believing Marie and not because she was not an honest person. In fact, she was a rock star in the graduate program. She just finished her defense proposal and was on target to finish her Ph.D. in less than two years. She had been published in two different top criminal justice journals. Both publications were with Bron, but she had another publication coming out in a month with Rot. I did not condone any form of violence, but Bron could get any woman that he wanted at any time.

I knew that his bank account and charm typically assured his success. I had been a witness to his behavior since graduate school. This was the first incident on file over his entire academic career. I had never heard any rumblings concerning his behavior. However, Marie was rumored to be grading all Bronston's assignments and teaching his classes when he was "sick," which was frequent. This was a known fact on campus, and Marie never filed a report concerning that treatment. I assumed that she endured his work system because she was gaining publications and perks. She was one of the few graduate students listed on his recent state grant. Most people would kill for one publication and recognition on a grant. Therefore, I hesitated to believe her now or wondered whether it was a result of something else between her and Bron. Bron was always going to be true to himself, but he would never cross that line.

Dr. Alfred Brown entered the room. "You look so beautiful. How is your day going?" said Alfred.

He moved into my personal space. I raised my arm to stop him mid-step. "I am fine, thank you."

"Your dress is beautiful on your body form," said Alfred.

"You should keep your mouth shut once Rot enters the room. Jo, you did not say that you are pitching both Brown and me to Rot. She is not going to go for both, and she is going to make you pick one. We both are skilled in the statistical aspect of the project. You do not need us both," replied Bron.

But I needed them both, Bronston for his name and Brown as a backup for the days in which Bron flaked. I took a move from Rot's playbook on executing a plan. She said to focus on the task at hand and always have a backup. I figured that I could bat my eyes at Alfred to ensure that he would work several long nights regardless of how late Rot wanted him to work on the project. The other trump card was that I was holding a secret about Alfred that he did not want everyone to know.

"There are benefits in having us both," said Alfred.

I got the feeling that Alfred figured that I would choose Bron over him. His social skills left much to be desired. Once at a lavish, faculty function, he only said about three words the entire time but laughed intermittently to himself in the middle of the room. Alfred's educational background was in Homeland Security. He was a well-known expert in his field, but he had never secured a state or national grant. He usually did not make it past the last round, which included interacting with the people. He always fell short within this area. Outsiders underestimated the socialization that must occur to get and keep an academic grant. Not everyone needed to like you, but the right people, especially when you needed their title and office header on a support letter.

About a month ago, I had a situation with Alfred. He pulled me close to him and tried to kiss me. I pulled away quickly. He had always been close to the edge on inappropriate comments, but never fully over the edge. Rot labeled his behavior as "yellow zone" sexual misconduct. She stated that his delusional interpretation of any situation and priv-ilege did not allow him to consider that he could be fired for invading my space and touching me. She and Bron witnessed the situation in the hall. This stopped the two of them in mid-argument, and they focused on Alfred and me. Rot immediately stopped yelling at Bron and asked Alfred to take a step back. She then asked me if I was okay. I stated that I was okay. She stared at Alfred for what seemed like two full minutes, turned, and walked away. Bronston warned Alfred to follow Rot because he knew that she was walking down to Human Resources. We watched her as she walked down the hallway and walked through the Human Resources door. We were both in denial of what was occurring at that moment; she filed a complaint.

Rot has both a Ph.D. and a J.D. I withdrew the complaint and framed the situation as an effort to kiss me on both cheeks. I tried to frame it in a societal context using my sociology degree. My chair did not want to engage in any type of complaint, and my husband was perturbed, to say the least, when he heard about the situation. He now showed up on campus at random times. Everyone was welcome at the university, but he was a very tall, muscular man that would frighten anyone upon sight. My chair typically ducked within his office upon my husband's arrival.

"So let me get this straight—you want Rot to get past his yellow zone incident and my incident. Okay," said Bron.

"Do not worry; Sarah will not be upset that I am on the team. The Human Resources incident is over, and that happened last month," uttered Alfred.

"Worry? It's not a situation of worry. She will be done. Does your limited scope of comprehension grasp this present-day reality?" shouted Bron.

"I get it," whispered Alfred, stepping back within the mid-size room.

"No, you do not get it. Rot's eyes turned red when she looked at you last month. You are not afraid of her? You should be. She filed a report on you. You're not mad at her?" asked Bron.

"She gave a presentation on sexual misconduct in front of a standing-room-only on campus last week and is giving one tonight in her graduate class. You are not mad? I just want to make Joanna happy," said Alfred, attempting to brush his hand on my shoulder.

"This is the plan, Jo, to make you happy?" said Bron, breaking the distance between myself and Alfred so he could not touch me.

I needed to divert this conversation to something else before Bron hurt Alfred before the meeting even started. I needed Alfred's connection to Homeland Security. The grant included a point system that gave points for including multiple disciplines. Homeland Security, psychology, and education were options on the grants, so I needed Alfred, but I also needed Pricilla.

Dr. Pricilla Appleton walked into the room.

"Oh, hell no. I cannot deny her expertise, but she cannot keep a secret. Did you forget about the holiday party? How many rumors did you hear from her at that event? Few people need to know about this application to reduce competition. She cannot keep anything quiet," said Bron.

I knew within my core that Bron was right; Pricilla could not keep a secret unless it hit home for her. She was banking on this grant outweighing her secret if the administration got wind of it. The university had just got confirmation about her sexual orientation. She had held this secret until her promotion to associate last term. In fact, Rot showed her how to cloak it under a university policy.

"No, I am wrong. She did not inform me about a case being filed against me. She kept that a secret. She knew my name was on the Title IX form. She works at counseling services as part of her service to the university, but she did not give me a heads-up," said Bron.

"I could not say anything about it, or I would have been fired. Can't we get beyond this?"

"No," stated Bron.

Trying to change the subject, Pricilla said, "Sorry, I am late. I assume that I am the last person to arrive. No, Petrot has not arrived yet."

"How many people are going to walk through the door before Rot arrives, Jo? How many more surprises?" said Bron.

I knew that Bron had not read the application, or he would have had an idea of how many people could be on the grant or walk into the room, but I was not surprised about this aspect.

"I like surprises. I think you are doing a wonderful job, and the color you have on really brings out your eye color," said Alfred.

I needed Alfred to stop making comments, but Pricilla, on the other hand, assumed that her $2,000 outfit entitled her to special treatment and the ability to arrive late. She always sported the latest trend and let you know it. I could never remember one single day in which she did not work in the price of her outfit, family vacation, or her wonderful children, which you could also see on Facebook. She also tended to embellish a story and label everyone with a psychological diagnosis. The only other person's clothing that she mentioned daily was Rot's shoes. I thought she was obsessed with Rot, but her Facebook obsession was deplorable.

Rot entered the room.

"Heck NO. Two predators and a person that can never stop talking," declared Rot.

"I am not a confirmed predator or like Alfred," stated Bron.

"We need to keep this application under wraps, so we can reduce the competition pool, and Pricilla cannot keep a secret," responded Rot.

"Exactly," stated Bron.

Rot looked around the room fully to take in everyone. It was like she was considering the situation on a chess board.

"The name recognition of everyone is correct. This alone will place us above other applications. I am assuming that President Miller already agreed to write a support letter. Bronston and Alfred bring the same skillset, but Alfred has a Homeland Security background. I noticed this aspect in the addendum of the application. Which I guess you did also, Jo?" asked Rot.

"You need my name on the grant. And I know you hear me. You cannot ignore this aspect of me at this moment. My name recognition alone will place us on a certain level," shouted Bron.

"And so will YOUR sexual misconduct complaint," said Rot.

"Not after tomorrow," retorted Bron.

"You hope and pray. Judgement Day is coming," said Rot, talking to Bron. Rot turned back to me and went back to ignoring everyone else.

"I serve a purpose?" said Alfred.

"Please do not talk until spoken to, Brown. I can only tolerate so much of your voice in this situation," said Rot, lowering her voice.

"Told you," said Bron. Rot shook her head.

"Look, you have done most of the literature review with your last project. This would be an extension of your work, and it would yield so many opportunities for you now and in the future. Do I need to remind you that you are strategic and never let anything cloud a business decision?" I said.

"No, but Jo, you are crazy if you think I am working with the people you have assembled in this room. I have a reputation to protect, and so do you. No wonder the email did not list the entire team. Nice trick, but I doubt it will work in the end," responded Rot.

Rot turned and walked out of the room.

"She cannot walk around campus this late by herself. She needs her escort. She has a stalker."

"Who would be afraid of her? She is a survivor and a cunning adversary. I would be afraid for the life of the stalker. Remember, she taught the self-defense classes last year when the instructor got COVID," said Bron.

"She cannot be alone."

"I will catch up to her and try to convince her to join. I can do this. I want to do this," said Pricilla.

"Our fate is in the hands of a person who gossips, which is a trait that Rot loves," declared Bron.

Chapter Two
Dr. Sarah Petrot

needed to catch my breath after that ambush. The crisp air of the twinkling night brought a sense of calmness over me for a moment. Jo could be so infuriating at times. She should just follow my lead in most situations. I was going to get that grant, but not with that team. I could not wait to talk to her later. "Who is making that noise? I hear you, and you are not going to frighten me."

"I did not mean to frighten you," said Pricilla.

"You did not frighten me. Why are you lurking in the bushes?"

"I am not lurking. I know that you have a stalker and may need an escort. I came to help you," uttered Pricilla.

"Leave me alone." I almost made it to the door of the building without *the help* of Dr. Pricilla Appleton.

"Look, I just want to talk to you," said Pricilla.

"Why? I do not want to talk to you. I prefer to not have my business plastered all over campus tomorrow before 6:00 a.m. You know you almost cost me the Faculty Senate vote. It was a good thing your eavesdropping only impacted a portion of my plan. I should have realized that you were hanging around my office for a reason."

The Faculty Senate vote had been festering in my mind for a moment now. I often felt like wrapping my hands around Pricilla's neck to truly keep her quiet, but the law did not permit me to kill someone.

"I was trying to help you. I only went to talk to some of the board members to secure votes for you," declared Pricilla.

"Did I make this request? Let me answer the question for you. No. You never stop talking, and you want everyone to help you. Always the victim. You are only on the team because it serves you in some way, but did I notice the psychology, Homeland Security, OR education portion in the grant?"

"You didn't mention it at the meeting," said Pricilla.

"I knew my slight and tip of the hand to your narcissist ways would not be lost on you. You are distinctive in your field, but your discipline is not the only option on the grant."

"Are you considering the education option?" asked Pricilla.

"I am just stating a fact. The group would have to weigh the totality of the circumstances. Are you worth it?"

"I *AM* worth it," declared Pricilla as she was trying to lower her voice. I assumed that she wanted to calm down the conversation.

"I cannot believe that you want to work with Bronston. Didn't he push you down the steps at the last holiday party, or did you forget how I stayed with you at the hospital?"

"Joanna said that she did not see him do that," answered Pricilla.

"Okay. Joanna's undeniable beauty can talk her out of any situation in which she wants something. You could not have been that drunk. It was a short flight of stairs; didn't you feel some type of force?"

"That night is hazy. I had quite a few drinks," stated Pricilla.

"Let's go down memory lane for a moment. Bron only faked some form of concern when everyone wondered why he was so close to the steps and was not helping you. I was at your bedside when you were crying for your partner. I know the true you. My Aunt Marlene and I even helped your family until you got fully mobile. You know how many rides you needed to the office or to go shopping without your partner knowing?"

"I know you helped me, and my family LOVES the two of you and talks about you both constantly," responded Pricilla.

"Look. I have always helped you. I even helped you hide the identity of your partner. We practiced for days to ensure that you did not make a reference that would allow the university to ask any questions or be able to fire you on the spot. I owe you nothing."

"I know. You also know I need this grant to cover me in case my *other* situation comes out," stated Pricilla as she stared into my eyes in order to play on my empathic posture. I did not possess this trait.

"You almost burned me with that vote. I know who you are with all your flaws, but you crossed a line that day. I want nothing to do with you."

"You may be singing a new tune. You know I am not the only one with a secret. I heard things about your past in graduate school. I know you need this grant also," stated Pricilla.

"Really. You want to open that box?"

"You may force my hand. Joanna said we need your signature on the proposal form, or we also lose President Miller's letter. I will help her do anything to get it. If I get fired from this place, I will have to start all over again. I cannot do that to my family again," whispered Pricilla.

"Why are you whispering? Everyone knows your status now. And what does that have to do with me?"

"The political climate will not allow me to exist if everything comes out. I will be forced to hide my identity and teach on the high school level again," yelled Pricilla.

It was a good thing that the quad area in front of the building was empty and not littered with students due to the late hour.

"There is no need to yell. I can hear you. Yelling is for the weak."

"I know you erase people out of your life, but maybe a person made a mistake when they were actually trying to help you in order to get back into your life," uttered Pricilla.

"I refuse to respond to crazy."

"Is this the end of the conversation?" asked Pricilla

"Yes." I did not make a sound for two minutes. I just stared at Pricilla.

"You are playing a Jedi mind trick. I can play also. I have a Ph.D. in the field. You only have the undergraduate degree, and you call me a narcissist," stated Pricilla, trying to engage me.

I kept quiet.

"You are going to talk to me. It may not be tonight, but you are going to talk to me," declared Pricilla.

Pricilla finally got the hint and walked away.

"*Bye, Pricilla.* I am talking to you." Pricilla turned, stood, and stared at me for a moment and turned back on her journey to somewhere away from me.

This had been the most unproductive night. I had just finished teaching my graduate class, and I walked into the grant team meeting. And now, Pricilla just threatened me under the guise of her family, and I had to end the class nine minutes early because I had a stalker. The student received an F last term in one of my graduate classes. He never went to class nor did any quality, graduate-level work, but he assumed he would receive a high grade. After receiving a grade for an assignment in the middle of the term, the student had the nerve to inform me that I needed to rethink his grade before he went above me. I welcomed the opportunity to review his grade and past assignments with my supervisor, Dr. Peaboy. Peaboy—I refused to give him credit for his accomplishments—was upset that I was right, and the complaint never went beyond the department.

Within the graduate school, a student could receive nothing lower than a C. If the student received a grade lower than a C, they would be removed from the program for the next term. I was not happy about the policy nor the likelihood that the student could be retaking my class because it was required to graduate within the department. I fought to change the policy. I presented my arguments to several boards, and this got me quickly to the Faculty Senate. My strongest discussion point was how some students had an air of entitlement or a disconnect concerning grades, which should not have been the standard at the graduate level at Mill Run. The school was prestigious. The Faculty Senate was astonished at how fast I read and learned the policy structure and showed them that the changes must be made now, or other legal ramifications could occur. The university administration did not get involved at all. I knew that they did not want to get in the middle of the conversation or make the poor choice of picking a side other than mine. I really did not understand why people doubted me.

Before the start of the next term, the student got the letter stating that he could no longer come back to the program, and of course, he blamed me and not his poor performance. The number of emails and random appearances at various locations were maddening at times. Friends and family members documented incidents to increase the likelihood that the student would be arrested for stalking. The threats escalated in the past three weeks, so I had to get a restraining order. The student could not come onto campus because he was not a current, active student. There was no need. The restraining order also made it so that I had to work with Campus Security daily and more specifically Station Commander Lieutenant Pedro Alenzo. The concern for me was that I taught two nights a week. We decided that

Campus Security would walk me to my car on those nights. I just needed to call to get an escort.

We also decided to rotate my schedule. I had already set up a rotation, but ending class early was not on my list. I hated ending class early. Students paid for the entire time or even a few minutes over. And on top of everything, the class was upset because I let them go nine minutes early. I think one of them even cursed in shock, and he wanted assurance that I was not sick (e.g., COVID), nor that I would be in the parking lot watching to see who went home early. I assured them that I would never expose them to COVID, and I expected the same courtesy. I also suggested that if they wanted to stay, they could work on their final project and paper. Their response made me really dislike Lieutenant Alenzo even more. I told him that I did not want to give the stalker the satisfaction of changing my life. My point was lost on him, but it was not lost on his son, my undergraduate star student, Jonathan Pedro Alenzo. I often wondered if Jonathan was adopted.

I was looking forward to looking over the last corrections on a paper Jonathan and I were finishing so we could quickly start the new paper with Dr. Marcus Pimpleton from the library staff. I could not wait to get home, but I also had to call for my escort. To my surprise, Bron was at my door.

"Oh, no. What now? What do you want, Bron?"

"We need to talk," replied Bron.

"NO. I have nothing to say to you."

"Well, I have something to say to you," shouted Bron.

"Are you admitting that you are a predator?"

"You are going to stop calling me a predator, especially after tomorrow. I cannot wait. I am coming to find you as soon as we are done. You may have gotten Marie's lawyer ready for the proceeding, but you did not calculate one aspect." Bron smiled.

"*What?*"

"You cannot be in the room. Your puppet master performance cannot reach across campus. Defeat is in your future. You are a witch, but your witch's brew cannot turn Marie's lawyer into you," said Bron.

"It seems like you are a little nervous, especially since you are giving me this late-night visit."

"I just walked over to tell you to get off your moral high horse and focus on the business at hand. We need your name on the grant form," stated Bron.

"*YOU* need my name on the form to unblemish your reputation. Let's not mix apples and oranges."

"Let's also not forget. I know about your past from graduate school, and you will sign the form," Bron yelled.

"You know, Pricilla mentioned graduate school also tonight. This seems to be a running theme, but you forgot that *my* past is linked to both you and Jo. I wonder who has been talking? Someone is working an angel to benefit themselves. I just cannot place my finger on the angel at this moment."

"Why would I use my trump card?" said Bron.

"Is it really your trump card or a card we all share? You know, once you open some boxes, they can never be closed."

"Unlike everyone else, I am not afraid of you," declared Bron.

"I never said you were, nor should you be if you have nothing to hide. My witch's brew cannot impact honest people. You got me this job because of our relationship and benefits to yourself, but you changed the rules to benefit *ONLY* you and never the students *OR* me a year after I arrived. I cannot ethically stand in this position. I am one of the main faculty members trying to make the campus safer for all members. The optics are horrible. I cannot be seen with you."

"You never asked me if I did this," said Bron.

"Do I need to ask you?"

"And who asked you to be seen with me? I only need your name on the form. You can go back to ignoring me. This would be my preference," articulated Bron.

"You know your money cannot buy everything or everyone."

"You are one to talk, Ms. New Shoes Every Day and multiple streams of income," stated Bron.

"BUT I am not always thinking about myself. This is a constant that will help secure your downfall."

"You think you know me. I *know* the true you. You have mastered the skill of cloaking your true goals and objectives. Law school honed those skills. I also know what happens once you truly get mad," said Bron, placing his arms up in the air, indicating to me to deal with it.

"Wow, so you know me now?"

"I have always known you, even the parts you think you are hiding," stated Bron.

Jonathan walked around the corner. We both looked at him for a moment. How did he get into the office suite area without keys? How did he know that someone would be in the office area? It was past office hours. I sensed that Jonathan felt a little nervous because we both were staring at him and wondering how much of the conversation he had heard before making his presence known.

"I talked to my dad, and he said that you had not called for your escort. I was worried that something had happened to you, especially since the door was unlocked," said Jonathan.

"I guess someone took off the automatic lock. Did you send me an email and I did not respond?"

"No, I figured I would come over to the office to check on you. You usually work late on Monday nights," said Jonathan.

"I am okay. I had an unproductive meeting to attend before going home and picking up your notes."

"I am glad that you are okay," said Jonathan.

"Always within her shadow and never far from her side," Bron stated and smirked at Jonathan.

"I feel blessed to be working with my chair," said Jonathan, matching Bronston's smirk.

I was not his chair yet, but I was a fan of a person speaking their goals into existence. Jonathan was currently a shining star on the rise. We had two publications last year, one almost out the door, and we would start the new one within this week. I really wanted to see how much we could get done together in a couple of years. He loved to work on projects and was making every effort to increase his statistical skills. He was a breath of fresh air, but at this moment, the two men were jockeying in the small, narrow hallway for power.

"Your relationship will have a price tag in the end. Trust me," said Bron.

"I will gladly pay it for years to come," exclaimed Jonathan.

"Bye, Bron."

Bron leaned into me so that only I could hear him. "You are going to see me tomorrow with a grin on my face. I am going to pause and look at you for at least thirty seconds, so you can fully take in my splendor, impeccable outfit, and cheerfulness," said Bron.

I whispered back, "So many women are causing you so much trouble, and you cannot charm your way out of it. This must be killing you.

I may need the grant, but I will convince the group that we do not need you. I have a feeling that President Miller, another woman, will fall in line and away from you. Do not underestimate my ability to convince people of a plan that serves their best interest. You know that I *honed* my skills."

Bron brushed past Jonathan. I motioned and mouthed to Jonathan to ignore him and that he was upset about tomorrow.

Hearing my whispers, Bronston shouted, "I am not upset. I am confident that the day will be going my way. It always goes my way."

As Bron was turning the corner, Lieutenant Alenzo appeared.

"Good evening, Dr. Everstone. You are here late," responded Lieutenant Alenzo, noticing that both Jonathan and I were in the hallway.

"I had work to do," responded Bron as he rushed past Lieutenant Alenzo.

"Jonathan, why are you here?" said Lieutenant Alenzo.

"I wanted to make sure that Dr. Petrot was okay and that she had received my corrections. Our paper is being submitted tomorrow," said Jonathan.

"Why didn't you mention that you were going to check on her?" stated Lieutenant Alenzo.

"I figured that you knew I would check on her once I hung up. I was really concerned, and you did not seem that worried to me. I know everyone thinks that she can handle everything, but the escort system was put into place for a reason," declared Jonathan.

I looked up in the air because I did not want to be a part of the conversation, trying to make myself invisible. Lieutenant Alenzo did not know how to respond to Jonathan. You could tell from the expression on his face. He seemed to blurt out the next sentence that came to his mind.

"She had not called for an escort, so she had to be on campus. She follows the rules," expressed Lieutenant Alenzo.

"I just wanted to make sure," said Jonathan, glancing at his father.

I needed to neutralize the situation quickly. I did not want to have another scene tonight. I had enough tonight.

"You both can walk me out. I just need to pack up everything because tomorrow will be a big day. We submit our next paper."

"I am so excited! I probably will not be able to sleep tonight. We are really getting so much done in a short time period," pronounced Jonathan with a smile on his face.

"This is not your first publication, so you should be able to get some sleep. I insist."

"I know, but everything is going so fast. It is so exciting," declared Jonathan.

"I know." I was trying to shift the conversation from his father and put a positive spin in the air.

Jonathan beamed at me. He was aware that I only liked to be sur-rounded by positive people. He seemed a little embarrassed by his father and wanted to ignore his behavior OR for him to leave immediately. Jonathan knew that any problems associated with him this year would make me suggest that he wait until he entered the graduate program, which was next year. This would result in our working relationship ending immediately, although it had been proven to be quite profitable for us both. In fact, our relationship started because he convinced me to take him seriously once he hung up his football shoes.

I refused to acknowledge him until he took that step. To help him out, I did some research. I found out that the university could not take away his athletic scholarship, even though they threatened this aspect, but had to transfer it over to the academic side. I showed him that he had the grades, and he could do the research side, which he enjoyed more than football. He just never had someone believe and encourage him on the academic side. The alumni association was not happy when their star quarterback who took them to nationals for two years said he was done. I could care less; he had so much to offer the world, unlike his father. He must have been switched at birth.

"This is your third paper in less than two years. I guess quitting the football team was worth it. You could have done both," declared Lieutenant Alenzo.

"Dad, I told you it was worth it. Let's not bring it up again and not NOW. Do not start," said Jonathan.

"Let's go."

We all proceeded out of the office suite, but out of my back door. I had both a front door and a back door. I did not have a window or the largest office, unlike Bron, but I could come in and out without being noticed. Tomorrow was going to be a great day, but not for Bron.

Chapter Three
Dr. Bronston Everstone

TUESDAY MORNING

I had always loved the crisp smell of the air and not quite being able to see my breath during this time of the year. It brought forth for me a moment of reflection and a promise for the new year. Hmm. Today was going to be a great day. I was going to wipe that huge grin off Rot's face.

"Thanks for coming, Jo. I appreciate the support."

"You know I am here for another reason. And please tell me that you have another outfit. You know that you cannot wear grey. Grey is not your color. You have been trying it since graduate school. Please stop," said Jo.

"My suit for the hearing is in the car. Do you want to check it?"

"No, anything but grey is fine. You literally can wear any other color, but you insist on trying grey," said Jo.

"So, you came to campus early to insult me?"

"No, I cannot go anywhere near the Title IX hearing, but you have my support. When is your mom arriving, and how about your fraternity brothers?" said Jo.

"They will be here in a couple of hours. I figured your early-morning call and insistence on meeting now was because we needed to talk."

"Yes, stay focused on the plan. The objective today is to handle your situation. Do not focus on Rot. She gets under your skin," stated Jo.

"No, she does not."

"Okay. Regardless, she is the next step. Pricilla told me that their conversation did not move in a positive direction last night," exclaimed Jo.

"No surprise on that front. You have also got to handle Brown. I almost hit him last night."

"I can handle him. Do not doubt me. You would never give a morsel of doubt to Rot. Once we start, Alfred will be in a lab with a graduate assistant that will be right by his side and learning his every move. I already have this aspect in place," said Jo.

"Who?"

"Jonathan. Rot's undergraduate student. He will be a graduate student at that point," said Jo.

"I am not a fan."

Leaning forward and raising her eyebrows to the sky, Jo said, "Who cares? You will not be in the room."

"You know your beauty cannot get you out of everything."

"It has worked thus far," laughed Jo.

"I am also concerned about Pricilla."

"I told you that she has everything riding on this grant. I see her daily, *so much fun*, but she will hold the line," said Jo.

"The secret that you have on her must be good. She threatened Rot with our secret last night."

"No. She threatened Rot with a secret and one that is fake," laughed Jo.

"I knew you would never tell her the truth."

"I keep secrets and use them to *my* advantage. Why would I tell her anything of worth?" laughed Jo.

"You know Rot knows that Pricilla does not know the truth."

"I know. She was probably laughing when Pricilla suggested that she knew her secret," laughed Jo.

"So, why play the game?"

"I needed Rot to realize Pricilla's weakness and that I have positioned her correctly, and that she will not mention the grant to anyone. I know that Rot is concerned that Pricilla will blab our business to everyone, and that I picked the wrong person. Pricilla is not the only person in the psychology department, but she is the person for us. She also has the most prestige. She has been publishing in the top journals within her field," said Jo.

"You two are always playing chess."

"Not chess," stated Jo.

"No, I stand corrected—the game of life."

"Listen. Your legal team needs to bring this home, and you need to focus on the task at hand," said Jo with a serious tone and look on her face.

"They are ready."

"They better be ready. Why didn't anyone on your legal team consider that someone would think of university policy?" said Jo.

"Did you know about it before last week?"

"No, of course not. Rot is keeping this situation close to the vest. This is her specialty area in which she has a strong passion. Next week, she is scheduled to testify in the huge sexual assault court case involving the corporate millionaire," articulated Jo.

"I knew about the case, but I did not know about her involvement. She knows how to keep things quiet when she wants to keep them quiet."

"She knew that I would make an exception and help you, which I have. Please assure me that your team is ready, and nothing will come back on me. My chair is always looking for a reason to cause me problems or to get rid of me. I am not tenured yet, so I have to take him into consideration now," said Jo.

"I got you. They are ready."

"Mm. Food Service is starting to open its doors. I got to go. I do not need anyone to see me with you, and it looks like your fraternity brother is coming up now," said Jo as she walked away from me quickly.

"Dr. Joanna Taylor could stop a man's heart with one *special* look. I would be happy to die for that reason. Please tell me you're hitting that," said Malcolm Jennings.

"No, you know we have known each other since graduate school. She is married now. She just wanted to talk about a research project before the day got started."

"Great. You are focused on your work and not Petrot," stated Malcolm.

"I am not focused on her. She cannot be in the room. It would be a conflict of interest. She would be taking a stance against the university. She would never cross that line."

"So, I will not see her today? Who is covering your classes today? It is not Petrot, is it? I know she is in your department, and she would jump at the opportunity to cover your classes," said Malcolm.

"Heck no to all your questions, and Melvin is covering my classes. This is how he is showing me his support. And why are you here so early?"

"I am your line brother. We are walking in and walking out together today with a victory. Marie is not going to ruin your life," said Malcolm with intensity as he pulled his coat fully closed. The breeze of the air was starting to reduce the temperature.

We walked to my office within the criminal justice suite, and of course, my fraternity and family were already waiting for me, even my mom. I had not planned on being on stage for everyone this early in the morning. I had not gotten on my hearing suit yet.

The vibe in the office was hopeful and crowded. Everyone was trying to make me feel relaxed even though today was going to be long. We focused on everything else except the hearing, but then Rot arrived after I was in the office for about an hour. She always came into the office early, but often opted to use her back door. I guess she wanted to make sure I knew she was in the department wing. I had a feeling she did not expect the level of support for me this early in the morning. One of my line brothers' spouses had put out a spread so no one would get hungry, which was offered to anyone that entered the office space, even Rot.

"Rot, would you like something to eat? I have not seen you in such a long time. B told me that he had helped you get this job," said my mother.

"No, thank you. Yes, ma'am, he did help me get this job. You look younger each time I see you. How are your grandchildren doing? I heard one got accepted to Princeton," said Rot, eyeing me.

"They are all doing well," said Mom.

Rot scanned the room for a moment and found her target and said, *"Good morning, Malcolm."*

"Morning, Sarah," replied Malcolm.

Rot refused to let Malcolm call her Rot. He *might* use Petrot or Sarah, only. It was a long and sordid story.

Turning back to my mother, Rot said, "It is unfortunate that you all cannot go into the room to show your support." Rot made a guess that I had not informed my family and friends about this aspect. She was right.

"Is this true?" asked Malcolm and my mom inquisitively.

"No. I had no idea that everyone was coming this early or wanted to come to everything, but I appreciate the support. Only my lawyers can come in with me, but they did designate a room for anyone to wait that wanted to support me. The objective is to protect my rights and the student's rights."

Feeling satisfied of her small triumph and having a slight smile on her face, Rot said, "I have to go, but have a *blessed* day."

"Will you be in the room to show support?" asked my mother.

"You know your son and I have a long history, but I have a full schedule of teaching today," articulated Rot.

"You are covering his classes also, right? You know teaching is not his strong suit. He would not trust his work to just anyone," said my mother.

"No, Peaboy is doing that aspect for him," said Rot.

"Who is Peaboy, B? Why didn't you ask Rot? You need to focus on today and not worry about anything else," said my mom in an upset tone, which made everyone in the room lower their conversations. They wanted to hear the response but did not want to give the impression of entering the conversation; that would be rude.

Rot responded quickly and said, "Dr. Peaboy is our boss. He has it covered."

"Okay, if you say so. I trust you," said Mom as she gave me a big hug.

"Do not worry. Your son has assured me that he will find me once everything is over and give me *all* the details," said Rot.

No one moved while my mother and Rot had their exchange. Malcolm just stared at Rot intensely. I preferred my mother to be in the dark, and obviously, so did Rot. For some reason, Rot could do no wrong in my mother's eyes since graduate school.

Our relationship began as a result of a system in which our advisor placed people into pairs. You had to work with your partner in order to survive and advance. Rot showed me this aspect after the first month. She begged me to trust her, and her plan would yield publication resources for us in seven months. She did it after six.

I started seeing the spoils of our investment after two months. We were one of the first graduate pairs to have a publication with our advisor that term. We started getting invited to faculty events and were provided more funding than our colleagues. Of course, this was not broadcasted to anyone, especially not by Rot. Our advisor never did any work. Rot handled the classes because teaching came easily to her, and she really did not want to deal with my incompetence (her words) in this area.

She was quite direct about her feelings, especially when it came to work, but it was like she was a duck in water when it came to teaching. Students started requesting her classes, which of course were under the name of our advisor. It was a well-known fact that he never taught any of his classes once Rot arrived and he figured out her skillset. I hustled in the library with the help of several of my female friends to complete my portion of the research. I never missed a deadline. I recall once suggesting that I might be a little late on a deadline and later questioned whether Rot was seriously pondering killing me in the library at that moment or at my home. Rot was maintaining classes and the other portions of the research projects, so maintaining my obligations was my only option in her eyes.

She determined and outlined our plans since the university had linked us together. She did not want to be under the thumb of our advisor for longer than a moment. He was manipulating the system, and she could do nothing about it. She looked at several university policies, but we had limited resources as graduate students. I often saw him at different criminal justice conferences, and he asked about Rot; he called her Dr. Petrot. He would never make the mistake of using her first name even when we were in graduate school. It was Ms. Petrot. I thought he even shed a tear when we left, but not for me but because we helped him finish two more articles and a book. Rot made sure our names were in the publications and mentioned in the book. We got credit for writing a chapter, and so did Joanna. But we did the entire project. It was normal procedure for graduate students to look up material and help with the editing. The editing term was ambiguous. Rot also sent me out to do all the presentations on the local and national level. Unknown to Rot, I could travel with my lady friends. The school paid for the hotel and my trip; she made sure of this aspect. I would only have to pay for my guest. I happily made that happen. She knew that my charismatic charm would get both our names out regardless of if she was in attendance. She realized quickly that name recognition increased a person's likelihood of publication, especially when the paper was in the initial stages at the editor's desk. If the editor recognized or thought she recognized the name, she would be more likely to move the paper forward for review.

Her compulsive nature outlined everything until graduation day. We graduated ahead of schedule. Rot read the graduate policy manual and found a loophole that would help not only us, but anyone that followed, which happened to be Jo. The person just had to know about the loophole. The bones shared between Jo and Rot were endless, and they would ultimately do anything to help each other. They just always played on some type of game board. My mother loved and credited Rot for my stellar graduate career. My mother wanted the two of us to come home to Mill Run University. She told me that she never saw me work as hard, and she was upset, to say the least, when Rot decided to take a moment to focus on her legal options. Rot had made her mark then and at this moment, but I was going to have the last laugh before the end of the day.

"Mom, I need to get dressed in my office. I want to be ready for the day."

I watched Rot hurry to her office and quickly reemerge. I caught her eye and smirked at her because I did not want my mother to notice anything. I knew she was going to class because she was carrying her blue Vera bag, but I did not see her snack bag. I guessed she was not holding any study sessions today or had any meetings after class.

"Get that woman out of your head," declared Malcolm.

"I am not worried about her. I am focused on today."

Malcolm walked over to my shelf. He took a framed picture off the back portion of the shelf.

"Why haven't you burned this yet?" asked Malcolm.

"Jo is in the picture also. I thought you would *die* for a moment with Jo. The picture is part of my past. A moment in time. A designation of hope."

"This is my point exactly. You are holding on to graduate school. Sarah is helping the other side," uttered Malcolm.

"Is Rot helping the other side, or is my legal team lacking because they did not consider university policy?"

"I do not see Sarah giving *you* any words of wisdom," stated Malcolm.

"You know we do not have that relationship anymore."

"Just think, you got her this job," proclaimed Malcolm.

"The setup did start out golden."

"But you refused to bend to her will. She needed to follow your directions," declared Malcolm.

"And Rot is really good at following directions, especially when she thinks she is right?"

"She can never follow anyone. You set the tone for the criminal justice department," said Malcolm.

"The tone?"

"Yes, the tone. Sarah gets rid of anyone that does not bend or looks for a policy to make the person bend," stated Malcolm.

"Hence your lack of a relationship with her." I was trying to lighten the mood, but Malcolm seemed to be getting madder as the conversation moved on. He did not want to focus on Rot, but she seemed to be the focus of this conversation.

"You know that I would do anything for you, but I draw the line at her," said Malcolm.

"Okay. Did you draw the line before or after she reduced my presence with you?"

"Look, I am not going down memory lane with you. Who is standing here now willing to do anything for you?" stated Malcolm proudly.

"My line brother. I appreciate you coming to my side."

"Always! Look, we will hold down the fort while you get dressed. I am going to place this picture in the trash, and do not take it out," stated Malcolm.

I removed the picture from the trash once Malcolm had shut the door and placed it in its position on the shelf. We all had drifted off the plan from this picture, but we never let the collective truly fall regardless of the consequences of everyone else around us, especially Rot, but my situation was a point of contention for her. I wished she would take a moment and listen to me.

Chapter Four
Dr. Sarah Petrot

I could not believe that Bron's family brought a huge spread that included various types of breads to the criminal justice office. You would think that we were celebrating an award for Bron versus him being accused of sexual misconduct. I needed to get to class. The party for Bron in the office was throwing my day off. The packed hallway filled with students and chatter could not overshadow the distinct beauty of Jo.

"You know I only have a few minutes."

"Good morning to you, Rot," said Jo.

"Arrived at campus early today? Your first class does not start until eleven. You know I caught your little joke sent to me by Pricilla, so what lie did you tell her? It only took me a few seconds, but I assumed that you wanted me to play along and confirm that she knew a secret that I wanted to hide."

"It is for me to know and you to figure out the secret," said Jo.

"Do I really think I care about the content?"

"No, but I knew that you would appreciate the move," laughed Jo.

"It was funny. I almost threw it back in her face. Your persona *fools* everyone, but you are the person with the cold heart." I whispered this sentence to Jo because we were in the hallway, and I really could not tell who was listening to our conversation, nor did I underestimate people listening to others' conversation.

"Look, Pricilla has the most prestige at the moment," whispered Jo, matching my level.

"The most prestigious person does not always come without problems—or let's say this. People should opt to minimize their problems. I think you have bitten off more than you can handle, and what is the deal with Brown?"

"You and Bron have little faith in me. Alfred just needs to sign the form. You will never see him if you do not want to. I will make sure of that aspect," roared Jo quickly.

"Still with Camp Bron? I never see Alfred anyway. He does not exist in my world now."

"You know, people keep disappearing in your world, but exist in the real world," said Jo as her beauty parted the sea of students trying to get to class.

"We all construct our own reality. I just make people aware of mine. I do not have time for this type of conversation. I need to go and start this class. You know that I hate to start class late or end early."

"I know," replied Jo.

"I also know what you did for Bron, and you just tried to ignore my previous question just now. Here is a direct one. Did his law firm put you on a retainer? I know it took you a minute to find *all* his previous students, and especially ones that would have something positive to say. Did you do the interviews to ensure their positive statements?"

"Are you upset that you missed it?" said Jo.

"Always so confident, but you never account for Plan B, C, or D."

Out of the corner of my eye, I noticed Marie walking to her first class with her head held high. She was quiet, but the looks from the other students could make anyone cringe. She had become the student that was trying to ruin Dr. Everstone's life, or at least his fraternity was trying to paint that narrative. The campus had been covered with flyers of her and at the bottom the statement: LIAR. I gave her credit for holding her head up. Student Services removed the flyers every day, but they appeared every morning. The other aspect that was interesting to me was that Campus Security could not catch the culprits.

I moved my gaze quickly to return to my conversation with Jo. I did not want anyone to see me making eye contact with her or get the impression that I had involved myself in her case.

"You cannot save the world, Rot, and why account for another plan when you have considered all forms of divergence?" stated Jo.

"Wow…"

"Bron and his legal team know about the university policy, angel. Just admit that you have some cracks in your argument," said Jo.

"Bronston yelled about it all last week, so I knew. He could never keep quiet about anything that makes him mad. I do have some cracks, but you do not see them. And I certainly do not have a crack labeled Bronston."

"You once had one. A large one in fact," said Jo.

"Long time ago, but I stopped letting him onto the board. The days are coming down to picking a side, Jo."

"You know that there can be more than one side to a story, and you are not the judge to make that decision," stated Jo.

"Oh, so we believe in justice now?"

"I believe in justice and listening to both sides," said Jo.

"Oh, so you are taking the high road now and not using your beauty?"

"I just wanted to make sure that Bron has a fighting chance. Your help on the other side lessened his odds of coming out on top and being able to participate in this grant or even being able to start playing the game of life. You know that this situation could escalate," articulated Jo.

"You cannot confirm that I helped the other side."

"With you, never," stated Jo.

"I did not help the other side directly. And you are acting like he owns the game board."

"Nice play on words. No one owns the board. Just the illusion that someone can own it," proclaimed Jo.

"He thinks he owns it. Why call for a hearing if the case was not true? Most cases are resolved quietly in the president's office."

"You know that he was forced to take this route," asserted Jo.

"No, he opted for a legal team bluff, and the president called him on it."

"No, he had no option," said Jo.

"Was he really forced, OR has he now decided to burn down the place if he does not get his way? He does not want to be embarrassed in front of his precious fraternity brothers, and I guess you."

"Flashback from graduate school?" asked Jo.

"This has nothing to do with that time period."

"Look, just the mention of this situation has impacted his reputation. He has never had anyone make a claim before now. His track record is solid. Even you cannot ignore this aspect," said Jo.

"Neither his publication record, his money, nor a lack of a claim can help him now. Open your eyes."

"My eyes are wide open," articulated Jo.

"You are making choices now, and your flair for the dramatics is not helping the situation. At least I can go to sleep knowing that I am on the right side of justice, and I received no benefit."

"Are you sure?" said Jo.

"He is still going to lose today. Or let's say the day is not totally going to go in his favor."

The crowdedness of the hallway was lessening because most students had made it to their destination.

"Good morning, Dr. Petrot. Here are your notes for this lecture and the lecture later today. I am looking forward to your talk about 'yellow zone' sexual misconduct. I had a moment to look up some more citations," said Jonathan.

"It looks like fifteen more citations. It took you more than a moment. Thank you, Jonathan. I will see you in class."

"I like the new shadow. He is upright, eager, and he overprepares for a situation. You must be loving this aspect," said Jo, walking in the opposite direction. I turned around quickly, expecting to walk into my class, but I bumped into Pricilla.

"Sorry, I bumped into you," said Pricilla.

"It is a big hallway. I can see how we can easily bump into each other."

"I am sorry. Good morning. I hope I did not upset you last night. I think our conversation went in the wrong direction. I talked to Jo about it last night, and she suggested that I find you early this morning before your class," said Pricilla.

"Oh, she did. I will have to remember to thank her for that. I must go teach now. This will have to wait, and it may not be today. A lot is going on today."

I walked into the fifty-minute lecture hall, giving my best presentation of self, but feeling a sense that the campus was going to be transitioning into a dark form as the day went along. I ended the lecture by reminding the students that they had a mini-assignment due at the end of the week, and I was holding two study sessions today.

"I really enjoyed the lecture, Dr. Petrot," said Jonathan.

"I appreciate the kind words, but you have the job. You are the first undergraduate student to work for me."

"No, I really enjoyed it," Jonathan stated as we walked out the door and into Marcus.

"Okay, Jonathan. Good morning, Dr. Pimpleton." I shifted my gaze to Marcus.

"Good morning, Marcus. I mean, Dr. Pimpleton," said Jonathan as I gave him an unfavorable look for calling Dr. Pimpleton Marcus.

"I have the research articles that you wanted me to find for the next publication, Dr. Pimpleton. They are in the bottom of my bag at the moment. I came back to the library to make sure that I was ahead of the deadlines that you and Dr. Petrot outlined for me," stated Jonathan.

"I know that you both are submitting an article today. I could have waited for this information," said Marcus.

"I just want to make sure that I am being a good team member," said Jonathan.

"Jonathan, you know that you can go home, right?"

"I just want to make sure that you both are happy with my performance. It is important to me," articulated Jonathan.

"You are ahead of schedule. I think we are good."

"I think he needs a girlfriend," said Marcus.

"Inappropriate, Marcus. Please disregard Dr. Pimpleton's statement, Jonathan."

"Sarah, you know that she will make sure that he gets some sleep. My wife makes sure that I get some sleep," said Marcus.

"Inappropriate and why are you assuming that he does not have a significant other?"

"Do you have a girlfriend?" said Marcus.

"Do not answer that question, Jonathan. I will see you after my last study session today. Does that timeframe still work for you? I would like to submit the article later today."

"Of course," said Jonathan, ignoring Marcus and following my directions and making no eye contact.

"This will be our third one. I am so excited. This is turning out to be an exciting year for you."

"I know! Have a wonderful and productive day, Dr. Petrot. Bye, Dr. Pimpleton," said Jonathan.

"Why did you talk to him like that?"

"I needed him to leave. He had no intention of leaving your side, and I needed to talk to you alone. Jonathan is obviously obsessed with you," said Marcus.

"He is not. He likes to work. He is doing something that he likes to do, so it is not work for him. It is a way of life missed by so many people."

"He changed his entire life for you," said Marcus.

"No. He changed his trajectory to pursue other opportunities. He is just taking advantage of options early in life. Can you imagine starting at his age in undergraduate school? The tenure-track obligations would have been nothing but a short conversation. He will be chair of his department in record time if he takes that route."

"It sounds like you have everything planned for him," stated Marcus.

"No. I just show him options."

"It also sounds like you are pondering your review. Are you really worried about your own review this year? People would kill for your portfolio," stated Marcus.

"Look, you made this big production to get me alone. What do you want? And we have to walk and talk. I have a class starting in the next five minutes. We only have fifteen minutes between classes."

"How did the meeting go last night?" asked Marcus.

"Really. I told you—one step at a time."

"I know. I just wanted to touch base," stated Marcus.

"It was interesting. Jo suggested Everstone, Brown, and Appleton."

"What? Why would Pricilla want to work with Bronston? He pushed her down the stairs," asked Marcus.

"My point exactly."

"Brown may be a necessary evil now. He has extensive research skills, but I can do the work also. I have been taking some advanced statistics classes. Jo never really liked me in graduate school, and neither did Bronston. I always tried to fit into your clique, but it never worked in my favor," said Marcus as we maneuvered between students.

"Look, this is not graduate school. My strongest argument is that the grant includes several discipline options. We technically do not need both you and Pricilla."

"Pricilla has been active on the academic side, and I have been active only on the student services side," said Marcus.

"So! Please stop putting yourself down. It is not attractive, and Jo hates this trait. If you cannot plug yourself, then why should anyone help you?"

"I know you will have to talk fast to convince Jo to change her mind about me, but I know you can do it," said Marcus.

"Isn't this the reason for the visit? I told you that I had to meet everyone at the team meeting first. The next steps are removing team members and adding others while also getting beyond the Title IX hearing concerning Bron. I need to go to class unless you have something else to say."

"No," said Marcus.

After opening the door, a student yelled out, "Where is Jonathan?"

"He is not always with me."

"He often comes to this class to monitor it," said the student.

"Well, he is not here today. Let's continue with exploring the court cases assigned for today."

I wondered if Becky had talked to Bronston yet.

Chapter Five
Dr. Bronston Everstone

I was so furious that I placed myself in this predicament to be vulnerable to anyone, and now I had a request from the president to meet before the start of the hearing. My mother said that this was wonderful. We discussed my options for a few moments, but I could not shake the idea that in a few hours a group of underpaid individuals with less education than me would be determining my fate. The consensus from my fraternity brothers, which was growing larger every minute within the office suite, was that meeting with the president could not hurt my situation. My mother wanted to stay positive. She thought that our legal team had done their magic to make this problem disappear, for a fee of course.

I conferred for a moment over the phone with my lead attorney. He spouted legal jargon but emphasized that the university had not contacted him. He had made every effort up until today to settle the matter before the hearing. He suggested that I wait until he arrived before meeting with the president. He emphasized the importance of waiting and that I had no legal obligation to meet with her. The hearing was set to start in two hours. President Miller stated that I could bring my lawyer, but why would I need him? I had more than one degree. I opened the door of the suite to head to her office, but before going, I turned and looked back at my family and brothers.

"You can do this," shouted everyone.

I knew that I had to give them a sign of assurance. I gave them my biggest magnetic, Cheshire grin and held my head up high. I could not show any weakness to my fraternity brothers, but especially not to my mother. In her eyes, I was perfect since my father died. I would do anything not to tarnish that image. As I stepped into the hallway, I noticed that Jo was furiously trying to flag me down. I quickly caught up to her, and we ducked into an open classroom.

"Are you getting ready to talk to the president?" said Jo.

"How did you know about that? I just got the phone call."

"Pricilla just texted me the information, and I have no idea how she got it," stated Jo.

"And you do not think that she does not have a problem with gossiping?"

"Regardless, is it true?" asked Jo.

"Yes."

"Where is your lawyer?" asked Jo.

"I am going alone."

"I do not think that you should go talk to the president without your lawyer," declared Jo as she started to pace around the room.

"Please stop pacing, Jo."

"I pace when I am nervous, and this does not feel like a good situation," said Jo.

"Look, I am not afraid of Miller."

"You should be. You have not noticed that she is starting to use more policy in her responses to everything on campus. This has Rot's fingerprints all over it. She has been walking around campus at weird hours lately. This has been the most that I have seen her in one term. She usually focuses on donors during this time of year. Wait for your attorney," said Jo.

"She had the option to settle this earlier. Maybe she is trying to settle this now before we start."

"Have you looked outside? This situation is getting a lot of media coverage. There are a lot of different new outlets on the lawn," said Jo.

"We did not plan for this aspect."

"I know. What did your legal team expect? And what did you expect once your fraternity plastered Marie's name all around school?" said Jo.

"Look, my fraternity has not been charged with posting those flyers."

"Are you really taking this stance?" asked Jo.

"I am not taking a stance. It is the truth."

"I guess *WE* are on the crazy bus now. Look. I think President Miller is going to try and make a back-alley deal with you. Does she know about the other job offers?" said Jo.

"No. I have been keeping that aspect quiet. I only mentioned it to a few of my fraternity brothers and you."

"I still think you should wait for your attorney. Where is Rot? I think she has something up her sleeves. You are underestimating her. She is furious with you. This topic is hitting home for her. If she cannot hit you directly, she will make every effort to strike you from the side," said Jo.

"Look, I am not worried. I have to go, or the president will think that I am stalling."

Walking away from Jo into a basically empty hallway because classes had started up again, I felt like something bad was coming, and her comment about Rot was right. I walked onto the presidential suite. The office was empty except for her administrative assistant. I assumed that the others were in a departmental meeting or doing something. The assistant announced my arrival. President Miller stood as I entered the room, but she had an unusual look on her face. This was an image that I had never seen before, especially since I was the person that always brought her grants on the local, state, and national level every year.

Gesturing for me to have a seat, President Miller said, "Thank you for taking the time to talk to me this morning. I wanted to talk to you without your lawyers, but I also need to advise you that you have the right to have them present."

"I feel confident in my skillset to talk to you."

"Okay. How confident are you concerning this situation today?" asked Miller.

"My attorneys have assured me that I have little to fear."

"Let me have you ponder a few other issues," said Miller.

"What other issues?"

"It has come to my attention that Marie's representation will be arguing various aspects of the Title IX policy, but also issues concerning the theory of a 'safe' and 'healthy' environment for the student population," stated Miller.

"How did you find out about this aspect?"

"I have my ways," stated Miller.

"You mean Rot. I know she has her sights on an administrative position once she becomes tenured."

"You seem confident that she will get tenure," stated Miller.

"You doubt it. I do not. Once she decides on a path, it happens, or she finds a legal way to make it happen."

"Let's start from the beginning. I want to make sure that you are aware of all your options before you officially start today," said Miller.

"I feel like we are backtracking. You could have done this dance at the start."

"You started our conversation with a legal team. The situation shifted with that move," said Miller.

"I needed to protect myself."

"Now, I need to do what is in the best interest of the university and remove the media circus off my lawn. They arrived early this morning to my dismay," said Miller.

"I had nothing to do with the media. They serve no purpose to me. In fact, their presence complicates the situation."

"Good, we agree on one aspect. Let's see if we can agree on some others," said Miller.

"I am open to this option."

"You realize that this incident occurred during the Biden administration, and The Secretary of Education in the previous administration amended the regulations to Title IX to *85 FR 30026-Nondiscrimination on the Basis of Sex in Education Program or Activities Receiving Federal Financial Assistance,*" said President Miller.

"This is how we—the legal team—were able to demand the hearing aspect of this process."

"This is also how you have been able to post Marie Walker's name," said Miller.

"I HAVE NOT posted her name or stated her name in any way."

"No. I am sorry. You are correct. YOU have not posted it, but I have a feeling that your fraternity brothers have helped with his aspect. The fraternity house on campus has been careful. I must tip my hat to your legal team and the use of the ambiguity surrounding gag order definitions," said President Miller.

"You refused to settle this earlier."

"I thought we both, now, are focusing on your options today," said Miller.

"Only *my* options today."

"Again, are you sure that you do not want to wait for your lawyer?" said Miller.

"I am capable of weighing my options."

"Let's go back to the issue of safety and a nondiscriminatory environment. This discussion point would open the floodgates to a review of every aspect associated with keeping the campus safe under Title IX. For example, what procedures we use, hearings, reporting, et cetera," said President Miller.

"How does this impact me?"

"The federal government will not only look at your case, but every case before this one and coming. Was I not clear about this situation?" emphasized President Miller.

"What are you suggesting?"

"Let me add a little bit more to the story. How confident do you feel again?" said President Miller.

"I feel confident that we will win today."

"I know that you have had help to get character witnesses," stated President Miller.

"Another aspect you gleaned from Rot."

"No. I am assuming that you also know that Marie did not file on the alleged date of the incident. She filed a couple days after she went to the counseling center," said Miller.

"I am aware of this aspect, and I realize that it will have an impact on this current situation, but I assume that you or your legal team did not consider possible other cases following this one," said Miller.

"What?"

"You may win today, but there *may* be other students ready to file Title IX complaints at the end of this hearing," said Miller.

"You are bluffing."

"I may be," said Miller.

"It seems like you are making assumptions. The first is that I will win today."

"I think you have a strong case for today. The fact that Marie did not file on the day of the incident will be a sticking point for many people," said Miller.

"The second assumption is that this win will ensure that others will come forward."

"They may," declared President Miller.

"If anything, Rot has taught me that a judgement in my favor would decrease the likelihood of another coming forward. If, and only if, there were others."

"It seems like someone else has been reading Dr. Petrot's work," said Miller.

"Look, I am innocent. I should not have to deal with this level of harassment. You realize that you are harassing me. Students can say anything. The key is to investigate and to not pick sides."

"Wait. I feel like this conversation has quickly drifted off course. We are only talking," stated President Miller.

"No. I have hit *you* with some harsh realities."

"Okay, so let me hit you with some. I am aware that two other universities have started to court you with lucrative job opportunities. You could technically leave Mill Run at the end of the term without a blemish on your record. And of course, I could get the media off this lawn today," replied Miller.

"How do you know about that aspect?"

"Faculty assume that they are the only people that can wheel and deal a favor from a colleague," said Miller.

"Why would someone want me with such a *tarnished* brand?"

"It is not tarnished *yet*, and some schools need your title and prestige to raise their standing," articulated President Miller.

"Now are you suggesting that I am going to lose at the hearing? My finances have ensured that this path is unlikely to happen."

"Let me keep going. Whether you realize it or not, most offenders have a grooming route when they pick a victim," replied Miller.

"What does that have to do with me?"

"So, if other individuals come forward, the story may sound the same," explained Miller. "Which they all could have practiced and had help from someone on staff to align this fictitious story."

"I did not interrupt you," pronounced Miller.

"Please continue."

"No one could withstand this amount of scrutiny, especially when their graduate students are teaching all their classes and doing the bulk of their research," said Miller.

"Another point from Rot."

"No, this is fact. Everyone on campus is aware that you do not teach your classes. It did not help that I personally visited your classrooms for the last three weeks and documented your absence," said President Miller.

"I was working on my research."

"This may have worked for week one as an excuse, but it is not going to fly for *three* weeks," stated President Miller.

"I am working on a few research projects."

"No need to explain this issue now. We are just talking," articulated Miller.

"I can withstand rumors. I have done it in the past. Attractive people always have problems. I am used to women ignoring the truth and creating their own reality. I just have never had a university believe the student."

"Per policy, we had to investigate the allegation," said Miller.

"But you could have squashed it at the start."

"People have been covering for you for years concerning various incidents, and my predecessor is gone," said Miller.

"You are not that innocent."

"You are correct, but I am ready to cut my losses. I should also note that your chair will probably be stepping down to become faculty only soon. He is creating an unhealthy, productive environment for the faculty and students," said Miller.

"You are removing Dr. Peaboy as chair?"

"I just stated that he is opting to step down at the end of the school year. It was his choice. The announcement has not been formally made to the campus community," said President Miller.

"The end of the school year would be after Rot's review. You are going to make her chair, and then she will be aligned on the fast track to this office."

"Dr. Petrot has a review this year. I cannot speak about that or the rest. I need to also state that your publications have decreased greatly, and your recent state grant was small," said Miller.

"You mean that my publication record has decreased in comparison to Rot and her publications done with undergraduate and graduate students."

"Dr. Petrot has nothing to do with this moment," said President Miller.

"Really. A woman that is overproducing in my mind because she does not sleep has nothing to do with this conversation. You must be jumping for joy since her work includes working with students. I know you are advertising her performance to alumni, parents, and donors at every country club event in the state."

"I often forget that your income level is not like other faculty, and you hear things at social events. Look, we are going off track," stated Miller.

"Rot is a person that you will owe."

"I owe her nothing. I am always in control," stated Miller.

"You think you are in control. This is the illusion and sense of security that she creates for people. There is a *price* to pay for her knowledge. She will ultimately have your job in less than three years, Mark my words. You are on her board of life."

"Her board of life?" asked Miller.

"See, you are oblivious to your own situation."

"I am quite aware of where I am standing," declared President Miller.

"Okay, ponder this. WE have had a solid relationship for two years. I have helped you secure funding from various sources on various levels. Does that go out the window now?"

"To be honest, which I will deny, I have been covering for you also," said Miller.

"So, is this all about the university brand? You are concerned that I will impact your bottom line, and Rot promises a larger bottom line."

"That is part of it, but there is no need to keep someone around that is creating an unsafe environment for the students and causing all kinds of problems for me. People are on the lawn, and I cannot legally remove them," said Miller.

"What do you want me to do?"

President Miller leaned forward and said, "Step down."

"And do what? This does not strike you as a back-alley deal?"

"There is no need to place such a negative cloud on this situation. Take one of the jobs at one of the other universities," declared President Miller.

"Leave?"

"Yes. Did you notice that both positions focus on research with little teaching obligations, and you have a bit of a raise? I negotiated deals that would fit you like a glove, and there is no need to thank me," said President Miller.

"Thank you?"

"You are right. This would not be your style. Let me make sure that I am clear. I can make the hearing portion go away. It will not appear on your record, and you will take a new position. You can announce the new position and put any spin on it in any form that you desire. I will not contradict it," stated President Miller.

"Why would you do that?"

"I need the media circus off the lawn. I do not need everyone looking at how we handle sexual violence incidents, especially the Office of Civil Rights (OCR). This is a federally funded university, so this could open the door to the Department of Education, OCR. This situation is already affecting enrollment and our statistical reports under the Clery Act. I do not need this problem," said President Miller.

"What if I decide not to do this plan?"

"Okay. You are correct. You have a choice to make *now*," said President Miller.

I pondered my options for a moment. Why was Jo trying to talk to me before I went into this meeting? Was I missing something?

"Are you going to take the new job?" stated Miller.

"No."

"Okay. Once you walk out that door, we are done and on opposite sides. I will do everything to create a strong separate line between us. The two years that we have worked together have been somewhat fruitful, but our season is over," articulated Miller.

"I am innocent. I welcome the opportunity to clear my name. This is not going to destroy me."

"Sure, it is not," announced President Miller as I walked out of the door. I needed to talk to Jo, but I had to go back to my office. Everyone would be waiting for me to hear what had happened in the office. I hoped Jo found out anything to help me.

Chapter Six
Dr. Joanna Taylor

I was worried about Bron's visit to the president's office. Bron was losing it. He was so focused on Rot that he could not hear anything else. It was like being back in graduate school again. Once Rot said something, he heard nothing else. The obsession between the two of them was maddening at times. I came early to remind him to only focus on his situation today.

I needed this grant. The president was changing the rules on campus. No one was noticing how many people were being "changed" to other locations and positions. I had to get to my office so that I could get ready for class, but guess who was standing at my door? Pricilla instead of Bron. I hoped that he would be able to duck in before going back to his office after his visit with the president.

"How did you know that Bron got a call from the president?"

"Information finds me. Love your outfit," said Pricilla.

"This is why people run from you."

"So, it did not help Bronston to talk to you before he talked to the president. I wanted him to know that I was trying to help him. I wanted to give him a heads-up, so the two of you could weigh his options. I know that you are good friends," said Pricilla.

"Always trying."

"Well, last week was not good for him. He looked good of course. He can rock a crisp, white shirt with anything," said Pricilla.

"What are you talking about?"

"That's right—you and Petrot missed the action. He had a screaming match with Marie. He had found out that she had a publication coming out with Petrot in less than a month. Does she sleep?" said Pricilla.

"Why does everyone ask this question? She sleeps."

"You are BFFs," said Pricilla.

"You could hear their conversation in my hall. He stated that Marie should NEVER have been working with another faculty member. He trained her, and her research skills would have NEVER improved without him," articulated Pricilla.

"What did you do?"

"I could hear the conversation, so there was no need to insert myself. The conversation ended with Marie running off crying, Bronston slamming doors, and Peaboy doing nothing about it. That guy is a waste of space," enunciated Pricilla.

"He hates confrontation."

"Sounds like your passive-aggressive chair," said Pricilla.

"Please do not mention that man's name at this moment."

"Okay, you know Bronston was wrong. Students should take advantage of all their opportunities at all times. Marie's research interest aligned more with Petrot's work," said Pricilla.

"I know."

"On which part, that it aligns, or Bronston was wrong?" asked Pricilla.

"Marie enjoys working long hours. Rot attracts that type of student, so she should be working with Rot."

"Did Bronston know that I told you about the president wanting to talk to him?" said Pricilla, focusing again on Bronston.

"Yes, I told him. Let's change this subject before my class. How did your conversation go with Rot today?"

"I accidentally bumped into her in the hallway," mumbled Pricilla.

"You touched her? I give you credit for that move."

"She would not have acknowledged me unless I took drastic action. What's up with Jonathan? Of course, he was standing by her side, but said nothing. I have had him in class," said Pricilla.

"It is her new shadow. He knows to keep quiet, or she will replace him because he is an undergraduate student."

"I am worth a 'good morning,'" said Pricilla.

"I highly doubt he did not say good morning. He is very respectable."

"He said good morning, but then quickly stood at a distance without recognizing my true presence," stated Pricilla.

"He was soaking in it."

"Can you believe that he gave up his football career for her?" asked Pricilla.

"He made a choice."

"The first time I saw Jonathan was on the football field at a home game. You know he was the QB."

"I know."

"It was pure magic to watch him throw the ball into the air as the wide receiver caught it. It was breathtaking to watch during some close home games. It was like he was enjoying keeping the fans on the edge of their seats, but he always humbly delivered the ending with a win and a pearly-white smile," said Pricilla.

"I know."

"And he always looks good in anything, loungewear, business casual. Females and some males are constantly trying to get his attention," stated Pricilla.

"You are really up on the undergraduate gossip."

"How can you not know about this kid? This guy took the school to two championships within two years. We came from a zero-win to twelve-win season, so everyone was furious when he decided to quit. The tailgating parties have been horrible since he left. I have reduced my presence to only one hour. It gives everyone a chance to soak in my aura. Petrot also got his sports scholarship transferred into an academic scholarship," said Pricilla.

"I know. How did you know this aspect?"

"It is a fact circulating around school," stated Pricilla.

"Is this what you came to talk to me about?"

"No. I am just pointing out that Jonathan has no interest in leaving her side, *ever*. Is he working on the grant also?" asked Pricilla.

"This aspect has not been worked out yet. She has not signed the dotted line yet."

"Good morning," said Alfred, startling both Pricilla and me. He often took the time to visit me on some mornings to take an item, but I figured that he would not do it in front of Pricilla.

"Good morning," said Pricilla and I in unison.

"How may I help you this morning?"

"Did you find out any updates from our meeting last night?" said Alfred as he was roaming around my mid-size office touching everything.

"No, nothing new."

"We had quite a *discussion*, but it was fruitful. I think you did a superb job running it," stated Alfred.

"I think everyone is waiting until the conclusion of the Title IX hearing today."

"Today is going to be interesting. Everyone is buzzing about it. Staff, faculty, and administration. I went and had some food in the criminal justice suite. It was a huge spread that you could smell from a distance," stated Pricilla.

"So, you just walked in, Pricilla?"

"I did not get the feeling that you could not walk into the criminal justice office," stated Pricilla.

"Bronston did not say much to me, but his mother did offer me some food. It seemed rude not to take anything," said Alfred, injecting himself into the conversation.

"The area was packed with his fraternity brothers and allies, so maybe he did not see you," replied Pricilla.

"Maybe," said Alfred.

"I did, however, get to meet Bronston's mother. She drips of very old money. Did you see her outfit and the rock on her hand? Her outfit must have cost more than my pay for two months," said Pricilla to us both.

"She had on a nice outfit, but it can never compare to Joanna's outfits," said Alfred.

"Of course it cannot." Pricilla smirked.

"Are you always looking at someone's clothing?"

"No, but you must respect fashion and a person's effort to be stylish, which is not the reality for some people," stated Pricilla as she motioned her eyes toward Alfred.

"Fashion is not everything."

"Says the woman that can rock a paper bag and gain new followers," said Pricilla.

"I do take time to look stylish."

"But you do not have to make the effort. On a clothing note, did you see Petrot's shoes today? You have known her for years. Does she have her shoes delivered daily? Does she ever wear the same shoes twice, or does she donate them? She looks like a person that would donate them," asked Pricilla.

"I have no idea."

"Right, but you admit that she never wears her shoes twice," said Pricilla.

"Do you think the Title IX hearing will be done today? I would like for us to start working on the grant today," said Alfred, trying to change the subject that obviously got off track.

"Yes?"

"I love your eye shadow color choice today. It accentuates your pant and jacket ensemble," said Alfred as he was leaning across my desk in front of a picture. The picture fell forward on my desk.

"Petrot has that same picture with the same quote. It used to be on her desk, but I have not seen it in a while. It is from graduate school, right?" asked Pricilla.

"Yes, we took the picture close to their graduation day. I had another year. Alfred, please come back and open your hand before you place it in your pocket."

Alfred walked back into the office and opened his hands. He had my engraved pen with my name on it that I received at graduation when I got my Ph.D.

"That is not yours," said Pricilla.

"It was falling off your desk. I was going to move it closer to your computer," stated Alfred.

"Walking out the door?" asked Pricilla, shaking her head while rubbing her temple but making no further comments.

"I appreciate you thinking of me. Thank you so much."

"No problem. I guess I will talk to you today after the hearing," stated Alfred with a grin, ignoring the elephant in the room.

"My husband is picking me up today, so I doubt it."

"I thought I noticed your car in the parking lot this morning," stated Pricilla.

"No. You must be mistaken. I got a ride to campus today. I have not been on campus long."

"You are right. I must be mistaken," stated Pricilla as she sat down in the chair near my desk, realizing that she needed to keep quiet.

"Okay, I guess I will see you around campus," affirmed Alfred.

"Have a nice day. I must go teach. Thank you again for my pen."

"Have a nice day, ladies," said Alfred as he scurried out of the office at the pace that he had entered my office.

Pricilla turned to me and asked, "I am so sorry for talking about your car. Does he try to take something every day?"

"Next time, let me do the bulk of the talking when he is in the room. And no, not every day. I usually do not let him in my office. Your presence allowed him to come into the office space."

"Why do you put up with him? Rot is right. He is a predator or high on the list of a pervert," said Pricilla.

"Look, I need you to keep quiet about him taking items. If it gets out, we are done, and we will not have a conversation to resolve the issue."

"You know that I can keep a secret," uttered Pricilla.

"I said it once. I am not going to repeat it."

"You sound like Petrot," said Pricilla.

"No. I am just stating a fact. We have no time for mistakes. The reality is that people are attracted to me. Some people can control it, some people constantly buy me gifts, and some like to take things that I touch. He is in the latter category. I have been dealing with it since I was little and competed in pageants. It comes with the program."

"How many did you win?" asked Pricilla.

"Let's say a lot."

"I must admit. Your beauty is striking. I have had to stop myself from staring at you."

"I know. I caught you a few times."

"Please stop laughing. Let me turn back to Petrot," said Pricilla.

"Of course. More tea?"

"Another person by her side today was Marcus. I peeped him talking to her this morning. I thought you said the grant would focus on the psychology avenue," said Pricilla.

"It will."

"Petrot does not agree. I feel like she hates me after the Faculty Senate incident. The room becomes so cold when she is not talking to you," said Pricilla.

"You are correct. Her chest raises when she talks about it and you. She often does not sit on the losing team. You almost helped to make that happen."

"She has one mode, off or on. She also has the routine of ignoring people down to a psychological science with only an undergraduate degree in the area," said Pricilla.

"You should know how to ignore her of all people. Do not worry about it or Marcus."

"You know Marcus only has an Ed.D. and not a Ph.D. My degree has more prestige, and I have more publications. Both are the highest degree you can get in each discipline."

"I know."

"But did you know this? The unconscious distinction between degree levels is demonstrated by greetings. Very few people greet Marcus as Dr. Pimpleton; they use his first name only. Thus, most people do not respect him," stated Pricilla.

"Was that your degree talking? Or are you trying to impress me?"

"Just making a point. He acts like a lap dog when he sees Petrot. She says jump, and he say how high? I heard the three of them are working on a paper now," declared Pricilla.

"How did you hear that?"

"Jonathan is always in the library talking to my graduate assistant Jennifer Hill or Marie. I assume that the three of them will be working on a paper soon. I check in with Jennifer weekly to make sure that they include me, and my name is first. I never turn down submissions of a paper," stated Pricilla.

"Using a Bron move?"

"I learn from the best. Let me continue about Marcus. I really thought Marcus was going to quit when they did not give him the promotion. He had been the Interim Director for the longest time. He never complained about his treatment from his previous boss, but other members of the university community (faculty, staff, students) made some calls and complaints," said Pricilla.

"You are really locked in on the tea on campus."

"This is a fact. You know he is overqualified for the position. I could not believe that they forced him to interview for the job. I am assuming that it has to do with his relationship with President Miller. It is a mutual hate relationship. Once the announcement of the new director came across the email, I did not see Marcus for a few days. I assumed he was gone," stated Pricilla.

"I hoped he was gone. He had never missed work."

"Hope? Mmm. I heard that Petrot got him to return. Did she do that?" asked Pricilla.

"I cannot make a comment about anything that you just said."

"Oh, so she did," said Pricilla.

"I did not say that. You have got to watch what you say to people."

"Look. There are so many media outlets on the lawn. Students are having a hard time getting around the cables," said Pricilla.

I assumed that she was trying to change the subject.

"President Miller hates bad press," said Pricilla.

"I am trying to ignore them. I must go to class. I will talk to you later once we both hear the result of the case."

"I have to agree with Alfred. I do not think that everything will be done today. Do you really think that the hearing will be done today?" asked Pricilla.

"They have to be done today, so we can move beyond this step."

"You and Petrot always seem to have a plan. I wonder how Bronston fits within both plans," said Pricilla.

Chapter Seven
Dr. Bronston Everstone

The university picked the most obscure location to hold the hearing. I guessed the thought was to pick an isolated location to decrease the likelihood that someone would see either party. Thus, the building smelled like a boys' locker room that had not been aired out in a few months.

"I am sure that your legal team presented a strong case," said Malcolm.

"Come over here before my mother gets to my side. Marie's legal team had some really strong points. I am not sure how this is all going to go in my direction. They may give me a partial sanction. I am paying that legal team so much money. This was supposed to be over before it got started. I should not be standing in this position."

"Look, this hearing just has you rattled a little bit," stated Malcolm.

"You think?"

"No need to be a butt. I am on your side," said Malcolm.

"You are right."

"Get it together. Do not show weakness. You are Dr. Bronston Everstone. You are fearless. You are a world-renowned scholar. Get it together," said Malcolm quietly so only I could hear him.

"Look, I have it together, but the closing for the other side was written by Rot. It had her fingerprints all over it. The passion. You did not hear it."

"She was not part of Marie's legal team. I think you are giving her too much credit," argued Malcolm.

"I think—no, I know you have always underestimated her."

"I know she comes from money, but she is trash to me. I told you years ago to stay away from that woman," said Malcolm.

"What woman?" said Mom.

"No one, Mother."

"How did everything go? I hate that we could not be in the room with you," said Mom.

"This is not like being in an actual courtroom. The process has different rules."

"It feels like a courtroom process," stated Mom.

"Everything was fine."

"Only fine? I did not pay for only fine. Your lead attorney assured me that we would not reach this level. I am a little disgusted with that man at this point," said Mom.

"It was better than fine, and the closing statement was strong. Do not worry. Remember, she did not file until three days later after she learned that she would not be on the next grant that I was submitting. I have always said that this is about revenge."

"I know. I cannot believe there are people protesting. Malcolm was right. Your fraternity brothers should go out there and show their support. And this building smells horrible," said Mom.

"See? The fraternity would be happy to help you and do this. The ladies from our sister sorority offered to make signs for you. There is nothing that we all would not do for you," said Malcolm.

"No, I do not want to feed into the press. It is best to ignore them. I am right."

"I will follow your lead until the point I need to step in. You do smell this building, right?" asked Mom.

"I echo that sentiment. And the building does smell horrible. I will have to get this suit dry-cleaned today, I cannot wait until tomorrow," said Malcolm.

"We just must wait for the decision. We can wait in the classroom designated for my side."

We moved to the room designed for my side and opened the windows immediately. The room had gone silent for the last two hours. I assumed that everyone was trying to figure out what to say to me. We had been in the room for four hours total. My legal team suggested that the decision might not come until tomorrow morning. The wait was infuriating. I assured my mother and everyone in the room that the wait would be worth it. Occasionally, Malcolm would start a conversation about something trivial. Over the last hour, I felt like I could drop a pin in the room and hear it. As I stared out the classroom window, the lawn of campus was swelling with a rainbow of people. I wondered why so many people were coming to this building, and then I heard a noise.

Ms. Walker chimed a bell in the center of the quad close to the front of the library and across from the building in which I was standing. I could see her, and she could definitely see me. My family and fraternity brothers rushed to the window. The chime reverberated across the campus due to the location. The school was nationally known for having concerts in the center of the quad because of the acoustics. Then we heard the alarm from the library go off. It was quite distinctive and went off at least twice a term. Someone must have triggered it. The person had to purposely either open a side door or the back door. The last person had a huge pail of garbage, which I ignored until the fan started.

The person stood across from Ms. Walker. The smell entered your respiratory system and would not leave. We all quickly began to close the windows because the taste of the smell caused several people near the commotion to start to choke, and other displayed motions of starting to vomit.

The commotion made everyone pause that was not near the building and quickly come to the noise, once they realized that the incident was not involving a shooting. In the wake of the numerous shootings across the United States, there was an immediate response to start running, which I wished most people had done. Above all the noise, over a microphone, Ms. Walker bellowed that the moment represented a pivotal point in university history. How was the university going to deal with this problem? She then talked about how the distinctive smell was put into place because the response by the campus thus far was garbage, and we should all be sick of smelling it. Finally, she ended by repeatedly saying her daughter's name, while the person near the trash can started passing out flyers. Ms. Walker stated that the campus wanted to know her daughter's name and disregarded her right to privacy, so they were going to remember her name NOW.

Everyone in the room was looking at me.

"Sexual violence on campus is pervasive. 13 percent of all students experience rape or sexual assault through physical force, violence or incapacitation among all graduate and undergraduate students, RAINN, n.d.," shouted Ms. Walker.[1]

I said nothing, and my mother broke the silence.

---

1 Rape, Rape, Abuse and Incest National Network RAINN (n.d.) *Campus sexual violence: Statistics* https://www.rainn.org/statistics/campus-sexual-violence

"This is ridiculous. Someone needs to stop this. Where is your legal team? Why doesn't this protest reach the level of defamation of character?" asked my mother.

"She has not stated my name. She is within the gag order requirements."

Malcolm walked closer to the window and said, "Nice trick."

Rot warned me that I would not be happy today. Was this the show, or did she have more planned for my day?

Malcolm walked back and stood closer to me and whispered so only I could hear, "Get that woman out of your head."

"Among graduate and professional students, 9.7 percent of females and 2.5 percent of males experience rape or sexual assault through physical force, violence, or incapacitation. RAINN, n.d.," stated Ms. Walker.[2]

"Mount up, gentlemen. We need to hit the quad now and stop that woman," said Malcolm.

"Stop. Wait."

"We need to address this now. She is not embarrassing you," declared Malcolm.

"No, brother. Take a breath and let me take an assessment of the situation."

"No," shouted Malcolm as he and several brothers proceeded to the door.

"*LOOK*, Campus Security has arrived. She may not have a permit."

"What?" asked Malcolm

"If you would have charged outside as planned, everyone would have gotten arrested, and the fraternity name would have been in the news."

"You are right, and this is not the first time that you have saved the house," stated Malcolm, still fuming.

"This was the objective. A move on the board."

---

2 Ibid.

"What?" asked Malcolm.

"Nothing. Just talking to myself."

Lieutenant Alenzo was arresting Ms. Walker, but not the person who was working the fan. I realized that the person was in a hooded jacket and could now be anyone in the crowd. Ms. Walker was profusely smiling for the cameras and taking pictures.

"The noise—chime and alarm—was purposefully put into place so that I could disrupt the day, and I am going to continue until I receive justice for my only child," shouted Ms. Walker.

There was a knock at the door. A student walked into the room. I was hoping that they had decided the outcome.

"A decision has *not* been made. In light of the incident on the lawn, the session has been ended for now, per orders from President Miller and the board members," said the student.

"What?" asked Malcolm.

Everyone was shouting some form of, "This is crazy."

"Let me talk to my lawyers first before everyone goes off the deep end."

"Handle this, or I will!" I knew that the statement came from my mother. She has never embarrassed me in public, but I feared that she could not control herself and had a knee-jerk moment. I also realized that Ms. Walker was gearing up for a fight regardless of the result, and I needed to stop her and really determine Rot's role in this production. This seemed like someone was trying to ruin my reputation and was not focused on the Title IX hearing.

Chapter Eight
Dr. Sarah Petrot

The brittle sounds of the wind and the leaves rustling on the sidewalk was not the only aspect one could hear on Mill Run's campus. In every kernel of campus, there was buzz concerning the Title IX hearing.

"Did you hear?" asked Jonathan.

"Hear what? You know I just came out of my second study session. Did the committee decide, or did the President make an *announcement?*"

"Neither," stated Jonathan, tilting his head.

"Hmm."

"There was a huge protest on the lawn, and everything has stopped," said Jonathan.

"I did hear some rumblings during both study sessions from some of the students, but I warned everyone that I would stop the study session if I heard another word off-topic."

"I assumed they got the hint, especially since the exam is on Friday," stated Jonathan.

"Yes, of course. What do you have in your hand? Is it for me?"

"No. It is on teal paper," said Jonathan, holding the paper to his side.

"It could be for me based on my research. It is the color of sexual assault awareness month. It is not the month of April, but I did notice that certain students are using the color on various items, for example, ribbons on their clothing, on campus as solidarity for the Title IX hearing."

"No. I am not trying to make a political statement at this moment, but it did come from the event," said Jonathan.

"I am lost. What event? The Title IX hearing?"

"No. It is a flyer from the protest which was outside of the building holding the Title IX hearing. It is filled with statistics and facts about sexual violence like your lecture last week. It even includes some of the data that you had me look up last week," stated Jonathan in a proud voice.

"This should confirm for you that you have the most updated information. I am proud of you. I would have been upset if *our* information did not align with *non-academic* individuals."

"I always keep you updated. I also noticed that the flyers and participants at the rally did not mention Dr. Everstone's name," said Jonathan, confirming his level of performance.

"It sounds like someone knows how to stay within the confines of a protest and to not violate a gag order. Look, we need to walk and talk as we saunter to my office."

"I felt like your lecture from last week was coming to life, but I was surprised when they arrested Ms. Walker and no one else," said Jonathan.

"Why?"

"I honestly do not think that law enforcement could find anyone else to arrest, especially when people disappear in a crowd," said Jonathan.

"Who disappeared?"

"I heard that they could not find the person running the fan or the person who set off the alarm," stated Jonathan.

"What fan? What alarm? I did not hear an alarm. Was it in this building?"

"No. The alarm was in the library. The protest included three people. There was Ms. Walker, a person running a fan in front of some garbage, and a person or persons who hit the library alarm," stated Jonathan.

"How stealthy of the people that got away, but Ms. Walker got arrested?"

"Yes. I was really surprised. I recalled your point last week of securing a permit to protest on campus to ensure or lessen the chance of protestors getting arrested or at least having some type of record," affirmed Jonathan.

"Maybe Ms. Walker wanted the focus to be on her and not the people that helped her put the protest together. Thus, she was the shiny object in the situation."

"Maybe. You also alluded but would never give legal advice that gaining a permit was not foolproof but helped with a defense tactic. The person could say that they were participating in a peaceful protest. You mentioned the importance of having legal grounds to help your attorney fight your case—within a hypothetical example, of course. I felt like the protestors took that step," said Jonathan.

"I was only giving you examples from past protestors' accounts of what they did to reduce their consequences. I would *never* give anyone legal advice without being retained as their lawyer."

"I know. I am assuming, and you told me *never* to assume. Campus Security did not know what to do because the group outside of the Title IX hearing was growing as the day went on. At first it was only a few media outlets. It became close to fifteen media outlets before the main event. I felt like someone made some calls to the various outlets," stated Jonathan.

"Hmmm. Really?"

"I felt like the situation escalated when the fan and alarm from the library went off and Ms. Walker got on the microphone," said Jonathan.

"A microphone would change the image."

"It did. But before she got on the microphone, initially, there was an inclination to run due to all the school shootings recently. Then the crowd realized that something of importance was going on and became curious," maintained Jonathan.

Jonathan opened the door to the criminal justice suite for me. His mother ensured that he had impeccable manners.

"So how did it end?"

"Everything is on pause. A decision has not been made," whispered Jonathan so only I could hear. I assumed that he was whispering because we had arrived in the criminal justice suite. We were standing in front of the desk of the criminal justice assistants, and many people were looking at us.

"Did you hear?" asked the criminal justice assistant.

"I would prefer not to gossip about the situation, so I am going to go to my office." Jonathan and I walked to my office. I kept the door open slightly.

"Dr. Petrot, I am so sorry I violated your rule," said Jonathan.

"Stop right there. We are good. She wanted to gossip about Dr. Everstone. Different playground."

"Okay, I do not want to upset you," uttered Jonathan.

"I have moved on."

"Okay," Jonathan stated quickly and took a seat at my table and began to unpack his bag.

"I would like to submit the current paper in one hour."

"We only need to look over the last few pages. I like the changes that you made late last night. When it gets accepted, we should very few edits, if any at all," stated Jonathan.

"This is the goal. I prefer to take the time now and have little to do later except the last overall check. Did you get my email concerning my new list of articles? I sent it in between my study sessions. I think the next paper can be done in a timely manner since Dr. Pimpleton is helping with the paper."

Jonathan kept moving his papers all over the table. He had a designated space, but it seemed as if he was taking over the entire table.

"I started on the list as soon as I got it, but I only got a few done. I had some other obligations today," stated Jonathan, still moving papers on the table.

"I just sent it to you a few hours ago. I did not expect you to start right away, but I did want to make sure that you had it. Do not take your eyes off your current classes. You are thinking about going to law school and graduate school at the same time. Your GPA cannot drop."

"I would never do that to you. I would never embarrass you like that," declared Jonathan.

"Good."

I was skimming my email and glanced at my Dropbox because his papers were driving me crazy on the table. I noticed I had two messages.

"Wait, it looks like you already obtained and placed a few of the articles within the Dropbox so I can read them tonight."

"I did. Did you notice that Dr. Pimpleton has not accepted his invite to join the group?" asked Jonathan.

"No. I did not notice it. Can you send him a reminder email?"

"Of course. Did you want me to send him anything else?" asked Jonathan.

"No, let's wait until Thursday. I want to do this last edit for this paper and get a gameplan for the next paper. I want a deadline date."

"If you fail to plan, you are planning to fail," stated Jonathan.

"You know that my chair in graduate school used to always say that quote, which is actually from Benjamin Franklin."

"I noticed it on the bottom of a picture frame of Dr. Taylor, Dr. Everstone, and you," stated Jonathan.

"That picture is behind both my recent teaching awards."

"But it is eye level when you sit at this table," stated Jonathan as he went over and picked it up and placed it on the table.

"I did not realize that aspect. I rarely sit at that location. You sit at that location."

"Sometimes, my mind wanders when we are trying to finish a document, and I look around the office. You do not have a window," said Jonathan.

"I know, but I have two doors."

Jonathan, now sitting, stated, "It is fine. I have a feeling that you will not be in this location long. And I want to make sure that I am on that path with you. I just want to make sure that I stay on task, and you are happy with my performance."

"I am happy with your performance. Your life has changed so much. You already have two offers at two of the top schools in the country, not including the offer here. Look, you are going to have so many opportunities that may not be with me."

"I would have *never* applied to those locations without your support. I know you are always telling me to look at all my options," stated Jonathan.

"Yes. These are your blessings."

"I know," whimpered Jonathan.

"Stop looking so glum. Your life is not horrible, but my table is looking bad."

"Did you hear?" asked Jo, widening my door without knocking.

"Jonathan, I need a moment to talk to Dr. Taylor. Can you come back in one hour so we can meet that deadline?"

"Of course," said Jonathan, gathering and placing his items in his bag. I got the feeling that he finally realized that it might have been bothering me. I liked things kept in an orderly fashion.

"One hour starting now. You may keep your items here but group them together."

"I will not be late," declared Jonathan, halfway down the hallway.

"You know he is just going to sit outside of your back door and wait," said Jo.

"Jonathan, come back. Have you eaten?"

Jonathan returned to my front door. "No," stated Jonathan, looking around the corner into the office.

"Please go get something to eat during that hour."

Coming fully into the doorway, Jonathan said, "Okay. Would you like me to get you something? You could not have possibly eaten with back-to-back study sessions. I also noticed that you did not have your snack bag in your Vera bag. I have no problem getting you something. I can put it on my meal plan. I never eat my weekly allotment."

"No, and the answer will always be NO to that offer. Please walk faster. The clock is ticking."

"Okay, see you in an hour," said Jonathan, walking at a faster pace from the criminal justice suite.

"You need to tell him to eat now," said Jo, laughing.

"No, he is just so excited. Remember those days? The first few publications and being happy to get products out. Or at least you were happy until you got the comments from the reviewers."

"So true," agreed Jo.

"Your skin never gets quite as tough until you start getting reviews of your work."

"You both have had a strong run lately," said Jo.

"You know I play the numbers. You produce so much, and something is always popping up."

"I still think he is pathetic," said Jo.

"So, you came to give me insults."

"No," said Jo, pausing for a moment. She seemed to be doing one of her dramatic, pouting moves. I was a little surprised that she was trying to use it on me.

"Okay, I noticed the dramatic pause. Should I clap now?"

Jo adjusted her stance and said, "So now you have insults. Sometimes it is hard to determine how to pitch a discussion to you. I was trying to determine the best route."

"Pitch it."

"I can see your fingerprints on today's events," stated Jo.

"I was in class all day and then study sessions."

"Which you happened to hold today. You could have held them on Wednesday or Thursday," declared Jo.

"I am preparing the students for exam two. You know the exams get harder."

"It seems convenient to me, and that you needed to give yourself an alibi," said Jo.

"Why would *I* need an alibi? I can account for my time. Can you?"

"I can account for my time," said Jo.

"Let's take a moment and look at some fingerprints. I feel confident that you have helped Bron all day and before today. You probably arrived really early to help him get mentally ready. No need to confirm that statement. I feel confident that I am correct."

"Look, he is a horrible person at times, but he did not do this. You must be questioning also. I see the graduate school picture on your table," said Jo.

"Jonathan just pulled it off the shelf."

"Why do you still have it if you hate him?" asked Jo.

"Why are you so confident he is innocent?"

"This is an area of concern for you, but have you ever considered that this crime gives no space to hear both sides? We are automatically stratified to either one side or the other. It is like you automatically must pick a team, and I think your research automatically makes you pick the victim's side. Which statistically is in your favor, but have you taken the time to talk to him? He has earned that option from you based on our history together," stated Jo.

"He is just using everyone to his advantage."

"This is nothing new coming from him. You just made him follow the rules in graduate school. He weighed the pros and cons of making you mad during that time and keeping you happy got him to *his* goals. Thus, he kept you happy. This supports my point that this man is not stupid. He may get caught up in you, but not stupid," said Jo.

"Or is he trying to make me happy now so you both can get this grant?"

"This is a surprise. We both want to secure our future. And let's make sure that we are stating everyone's reality. You want to secure this grant also. Regardless of the reason, change is the key. You once told me that sometimes you must make a person change for them to get it," stated Jo.

"Hmm."

"Think about it. He follows the rules. He would not cross the line. He has been around you for years. Why take the chance? You know that night in graduate school changed us all, but the three of us have always done what is in the best interest of the collective," said Jo.

"Hmm."

"There is no need to bring up that night. We all made decisions that night."

"That moment and that picture should remind you of the man he is and always will be. This is not part of his DNA," urged Jo.

"Hmm."

"He knows your passion with this topic. He knows that you would rain hell on him or anyone that crosses the line with a student. Hence we both know that you had a hand in today's protest. Do not deny it. You realize that he is fighting for his life and his reputation. His mother is here. He would never involve her unless something is amiss," said Jo.

Jo paused for a moment. She caused me to pause, and she said, "Think about it."

"Society always questions the victim and never questions a person in his position of power."

"My point exactly. You have picked the victim's side. Look, I know that others may come forward. And please do not give me the shocked look. I know you know about this aspect. I only ask that you ponder what students will do when they do not get their way. This is a new era where people will do and say anything to get their way," said Jo.

There was a knock at my back door. I figured she was setting me up for Bron to walk through the door. To our surprise, Brown was walking past my door in the sea of students.

"Oh, heck no. I do not talk to you. What do you want? And why are you knocking on my back door?"

"I noticed that Jo walked into the suite, and she has been in here for a moment. I figured that she was trying to convince you to join the team. I wanted to give her my support," said Brown.

"Jo, you are so good at assessing a person's character."

"Step in, Alfred," said Jo.

"So, you are inviting him into *my* office?"

"Only for a moment, I assume you do not want him standing in *your* doorway," declared Jo.

"I guess we are all at your party now, Jo." Brown walked further into the door, and I quickly closed the door.

"Alfred, hi, why are you here?" asked Jo.

"I really wanted to make sure that you did not need anything. I was trying to get your attention before you ducked into the suite, but you did not see me," said Brown.

"Jo, you did not see him in the crowded hallway at a functioning university."

"I assumed that she did not see me because I am short," acknowledged Brown.

"Yes, your height is the issue and nothing else."

Brown positioned himself to say something, but he uttered nothing. I knew that he would say something inappropriate in a matter of moments, but so did Jo.

"Alfred, I have quite a few things to do today, but I will touch base with you tomorrow. I will probably touch base with everyone tomorrow night. I plan on having a meeting tomorrow night," asserted Jo.

"I know the clock is ticking, and we must prepare the proposal. I have a few suggestions concerning the methods sections of the proposal. It should yield opportunities for both quantitative and qualitative research over a longer time period. This will increase avenues to publish for everyone involved in the project. I also contacted an associate within Homeland Security to write a support letter. He said he would help us," said Brown.

"Wow. You have done a lot in one day. Excellent job," said Jo, encouraging Brown. His face lit up with her words of encouragement.

"Why should I believe that you secured a support letter?"

Looking sad, Brown said, "I will forward the email to you after I escort Jo to her office."

"Jo, I did not realize that you were leaving, and you have an escort now."

"Alfred, I am going to talk to Rot for a few more moments about something else," stated Jo.

"I will do anything to make this project happen and to make you happy, Jo," said Brown.

"I guess the objective is to make you happy, Jo, but Brown, you must go. Jo has already stated that we have other objectives at the moment, and I see no reason to continue this conversation. I will expect the email in ten minutes, especially if you have it."

"I know that you are still mad at me about last month. Jo suggested that I talk to you, but sometimes it is hard to know how to approach you. I guess I am trying to approach you now," articulated Brown.

"Jo seems to think that it was all a misunderstanding. I think you ignore reality, and your status in life has given you that privilege."

"I respect your candor, but how long do I have to submit to your treatment before I become the victim?" asked Brown.

"Wow, someone put on his big-boy pants today. Jo, you put him up to this?"

"I told him to talk to you and to make the situation right. I have nothing to do with the content," pronounced Jo.

"You respect people who are direct. You may not like it, but I do realize that you respect it," said Brown.

"I do."

"I respect your mind and the way that you have honed your debate skills. You are frightening and inspiring at the same time. Did you see me at your presentation last week?" asked Alfred.

"I did notice you. How could I not? You sat in the center of the room, so I know you came early to get your seat. They had to add chairs to the lecture hall."

"I have never seen students flock to a professor like they flock to you. Your physical features are quite striking, especially with your short hair, but students are focused on your mind. They also clamor to get into your classes," stressed Alfred.

"This is exactly why I do not like to talk to this man, Jo."

"It sounds like he is trying to point out how people come to hear the context of your presentation and how they are *not* focused on your presentation of self," asserted Jo.

"Exactly. I thought I said that," proclaimed Alfred.

"Is that what you heard?"

"Yes. I am only requesting that I have a moment to sit at the table and prove my worth. I have looked over a few of your publications, and I am earnestly trying to change my behavior and my vocabulary. I cannot change overnight, but I am very willing to follow your lead," stated Alfred.

"Only a few?"

"Maybe more than a few," answered Alfred.

"Interesting. It sounds like I need to have Jonathan send you a list of articles to look over."

"I did notice him in the front row during the presentation feverishly writing notes," stressed Alfred.

"We usually go over ways in which I can improve delivery after a presentation."

"I just want to confirm that I know we all can get beyond last month. I welcome the opportunity to discuss ways in which I can change my behavior. No one is going to stop this team from happening. I will make sure of that aspect," said Brown.

"Let me think about it. I will consider the totality of the circumstances."

"I know that this will make Jo happy," maintained Alfred.

"And making Jo happy is the key. Send the email."

I started ushering Brown out the door and shut it.

Jo looked me dead in my eyes and said, "If any other person had made the same statements that he just made, you would have jumped at adding him to the team. He took a moment to be vulnerable to you."

"He took a moment to be humble because you told him to put on that show. It was a halfway decent performance. Did you practice with him?"

"You are not focused on the goal. This is your dream project. One that you dreamed about since graduate school. The grant that would yield research for years. What is really the problem? Is it because I put the team together and you may be wrong about Bron? This is the correct plan," claimed Jo.

Before I could respond to Jo, there was another knock at the front door.

"Did you hear?" asked Marcus, pushing the door fully open.

"I guess this is a revolving door today."

Jo looked at Marcus for a moment. The two were in the class behind Bronston and me. The three of us acknowledged Marcus, but he never hung in our circle because he was not in the Ph.D. program. The disdain that Jo gave to Marcus was similar to the disdain that the President gave to Marcus, but neither would mention why. They both seem to clam up and refuse to utter anything. Jo never treated anyone in this manner, and it contradicted her Southern upbringing. She did not live in the South, but her Southern grandmother who lived with her family had a huge impact on her upbringing. She would always inform me, until she realized that it was not working, what a lady would never do and how I needed to change my *unladylike* ways.

I was also surprised to hear from Jo right before graduation that Marcus was able to use the loophole that I found for Ph.D. students. I did not think that it applied to Ed.D. students. I never inquired about how he found out about it, but I assumed that she helped him since they were working on a project together. Once the paper was accepted at a top-tier sociological journal, she never mentioned his name again until she found out that he worked at Mill Run. Her demeanor shifted slightly, so I knew that the backstory for the two of them had to be interesting.

"I am gone," said Jo as she immediately turned and walked out the front door past Marcus.

"She will never add me to the team. I need to figure out another route to get on this team and to get Pricilla off," said Marcus.

"What is the deal with the two of you?"

"Nothing," defended Marcus.

"Her demeanor did not indicate 'nothing,' and I do not like surprises. What is the deal?"

"She did not have to treat me like that. I hate when she treats me like I am disposable," said Marcus.

"What are you talking about?"

"I really hate when she ignores me," blurted out Marcus.

"What is the big deal?"

"This was the first time that you noticed it because it was so blatant," said Marcus.

"I have treated you worse."

"The deadline for the grant will be here before we know it. How are you going to remove Pricilla?" asked Marcus.

"Why the sudden rush?"

"The deadline for the grant is coming up. Jo is never going to accept me, and you will not pick her over me," said Marcus.

"Paranoid today? And you are correct—I will never pick you over Jo, but it will never come to that scenario."

"She will place it in that format," stated Marcus.

"What is going on with everyone today? Is it a full moon tonight? I informed you that we need to get past the Title IX hearing, which should only take two days at the most. This will wipe out Bron and enable me to suggest a new slate of members."

My computer screen changed colors. It was an email from Brown. I guess he did get the support letter.

"Oh, great. Now your shadow is back, and we cannot finish this conversation. The three of you have always been the focus since graduate school. When do I get a chance to shine?" asked Marcus, moving forward in my office while trying to shut my door on Jonathan.

"What do we have to do with your shine?"

"All three of you have always gotten everything. You have more than one book, and I know you have another one getting ready to be published very soon. I have been working for as long as all of you," said Marcus.

"You can submit. Just like we submit."

"I am tired of keeping up this façade for all you Ph.D.s and being your research assistant with no credit on any of your papers, and always being ignored for any type of promotion," stated Marcus.

"So, obtaining articles for faculty, your job, demands credit on a written document that you did not write? Maybe the individuals that help with editing should also go on the document."

"Maybe," uttered Marcus.

"What?"

"When do I get a chance to shine? How many promises are going to go ignored before someone notices me?" asked Marcus.

"Wow, the real you just got to the party. Thank you for arriving. You have lost the good sense that the Lord has given you. You are so lucky that we are standing within this office and not off campus. I have so many more rights off campus. Oh, I wish I could use them."

"Joanna should have not treated me that way. You think you are so different than Bronston, but the two of you are just the same. You both use people," declared Marcus with a redness emerging from his eyes.

"I am?"

"You treat everyone like him but with a few more perks. Jonathan follows you around like a sick puppy. You are never alone. I would not be surprised if rumors started about you and Jonathan," exclaimed Marcus.

"She is nothing like Dr. Everstone, and I do not appreciate you making those statements," stated Jonathan as he stepped into the office and shut the door loudly.

"Jonathan, go get something to drink from a water fountain near the cafeteria."

Matching my lowered voice, Jonathan said, "He cannot insinuate these things about you. Do you realize how many people that she helps every year and every month, Marcus?"

"Jonathan."

"Dr. Pimpleton," said Jonathan painfully. Marcus started shaking. I think he realized that the conversation was going south quickly, and there was nothing to get his foot out of his mouth.

"Look, I was just upset. I did not mean the statements that I made," stated Marcus.

"You wanted to say it. She takes the time to work with students. It is so rare. This is why everyone thinks it is strange. She loves her work, and she surrounds herself with people who want to work. Nothing more. Nothing less. Why is this so hard for everyone to grasp? A professor that actually wants to teach and students that want to learn," said Jonathan.

"Jonathan. I can handle the conversation."

"I feel like I am a second-class citizen to some people, and no one really realizes it. Think about it. How many people on campus call me Marcus instead of Dr. Pimpleton?" responded Marcus.

"Jonathan."

Jonathan walked away slowly and gave Marcus a stare that could kill. I guess the second-class comment had no impact on him. It was as if he was having an out-of-body experience, and he was going to remove the problem, which seemed to be Marcus.

I lowered my voice further even though Jonathan was gone.

"You obviously think that you can talk to me in any fashion that you desire."

"Look, I…I just really got upset when Joanna walked out. She embarrassed me," uttered Marcus.

"Because a women has the nerve to walk out on you. No one talks to me in that fashion, not even my father. Rest his soul."

"Let's not turn this into something. I have been helping you obtain your journal articles for over a year with no complaints," said Marcus.

"It has turned."

"What does that mean?" asked Marcus as he stared to stare at the picture on my table. He was looking at it intently.

"I guess you will have to see."

"I guess you will have to see also. I think my luck and my relationship with the three of you just changed. I see something that most people from our past ignored," said Marcus.

For once, I honestly did not get the reference, but I refused to show it on my face. Marcus seemed sure about his information. He seemed to have a level of confidence now.

"I will be contacting all three of you shortly, and you all will be begging me to join the team," stated Marcus.

"When hell freezes over."

"I guess it will be frozen in a day. I just have to check something," declared Marcus. Marcus walked out the back door whistling. Fifteen minutes later, there was a knock at my front door. I assumed that it was Jonathan. To my surprise, it was Dr. Peaboy.

"The situation with Bronston has spilled over until tomorrow or maybe even the next day. President Miller suggested that you cover his class, so I need you to cover his classes. I know you can literally walk into the room and teach the classes without any preparation," said Peaboy.

"I thought you were covering his class?"

"I had several complaints concerning my performance today, and I have to attend a chair's meeting tomorrow," stated Peaboy.

"No. I refuse. Write me up. I did not offer this service, and you can get other junior faculty to fill his spot."

"You are junior faculty," said Peaboy.

"I am not afraid. Write me up."

"Of course you are not. You did hear me say that the president put in the request? She has enough on her plate. You are the most qualified, and the students will be happy to see you," articulated Peaboy.

"And why should I do this for you?"

"I have a feeling that you will need something from me before I step down and you take my spot as chair. You are a businesswoman. A marker from me will be worth it. At the very least, you can make the argument that I felt so confident in your performance that I allowed you to do me this favor," said Peaboy.

"President Miller told you what to say to me to make me do it. Didn't she? I appreciate the fake pretense."

"I am getting used to my reality. Unless I decide to retire," stated Peaboy, walking away from my office. I guess that was him dropping the mic in my face. Another head popped up around the corner. It was Pricilla.

"I guess you heard about Bronston. I also heard that you are mad at Marcus, and you are covering Bronston's class tomorrow," said Pricilla.

"Get out."

"I told you Marcus was not worth your time. You are the best person to cover for Bronston. The students hated Peaboy today. One student walked out midway in the class," explained Pricilla.

"Bye."

The day could not get any worse. The phone rang. Who could this be?

"I need you to come down to the office to talk to Lieutenant Alenzo and I before leaving campus," said President Miller.

"Of course. I will walk down now."

"Wait. It would be best if we all talk early in the morning. I will have some more information at that time. Can you come at eight?" asked President Miller.

"I will be in the office at seven. Please just email or call once you are ready."

"I will," said President Miller as she hung up. I was glad that the meeting had been switched to tomorrow morning. I would be able to obtain some answers on my end also. I needed to contact Jo. Marcus noticed something in that picture. I unfortunately might even have to contact Bron.

Chapter Nine
Dr. Joanna Taylor

I had to get away from Rot's office and the stench of Marcus. The image of Marcus made me sick, and being in his presence made me want to vomit. I would not have taken this job if I had known that he also worked at this university. He happened to not be present during my interview. I found out later that he purposely took the days off to ensure that we would not bump into each other. I was in graduate school alone with him for my last year. He had always tried to be with the three of us (Bron, Rot, and I) during graduate school, but Bron discouraged this aspect. Bron always said that Marcus was underhanded and had nothing to offer us. I should have followed his advice.

The three of us all did everything together. After graduation, Rot stayed for three months. We talked to Bron weekly, but Rot and I got close during that time. She crashed at my apartment. Because she was not working on anything, she helped me get ahead in my work and helped me prepare for my classes. She showed me how to present the course content at a steady pace so that the students were challenged but could keep up. The skills that I gained from her boosted my SRTE scores. I had never had low scores since, but we practiced until I got it correct. She could drive you to drink, but the results were worth it in the end.

She was a task-orientated person. I had the chance to visit her on a "reduced-working" day at the law firm of Wingfield & Wingfield.

She only worked ten hours that day and had only moments to talk with me. The pace she kept at the office was mind-blowing, and the rest of her staff fell in line. Yes, she moved up the ladder of the firm very quickly. This was why I was so surprised when she decided to quit her lucrative job and go back to teaching. I also figured that Bron had made her an offer that she could not refuse.

I missed them both so much when they both graduated summa cum laude, so I started hanging around Marcus. This decision had a ripple effect, but I had to protect the three of us. When I made the decision to protect the three of us without discussing it with them, I knew it would come back to haunt me. I just wanted to make one decision on my own, but the three of us were stronger together and volatile apart. Marcus had made sure that I remembered my decision, but every day on this campus brought me closer and closer to having to disclose the mistake I made to Bron and Rot. The day was turning out to be interesting, and not to my surprise, Alfred was pacing in front of my door.

"I sent her the information," said Alfred, trying to maneuver into my office.

"Who and what information?"

Alfred replied, "Rot. I sent her the email from my friend at Homeland Security."

"Let me make something very clear. You may never call her Rot. Pricilla does not call her Rot. Very few people call her Rot. I thought you were trying to get on her good side."

"I am," said Alfred, taking a seat at my desk. He was scanning the desk for the pen that he tried to take earlier that morning.

"Please call her Dr. Petrot, Petrot, or Sarah, but never Rot. In fact, do not call her Sarah. I do not need to have that conversation with her. And using Rot is a level of familiarity. You do not have that relationship with her."

Alfred moved forward in his chair, crossing a portion of my desk, and stated, "I would like to have that relationship with her."

I motioned for him to move back because I felt like he was trying to get close to me and said, "I would not hold my breath. Let's be happy with her interacting with you in a positive way during meetings."

"I will follow your lead. I will do anything to make sure that this project moves forward, but will the project not move forward without Petrot?" asked Alfred.

"We need Rot's name to ensure the letter from President Miller, but your letter helps."

"She mentioned my worth at the meeting last night," said Alfred.

"Yes. She sees value in you, as do I, but she did not like that interaction in the hallway between the two of us a few months ago. You involved her in our *complex* relationship."

"We passed that situation. When will she forgive me? I feel like she holds on to a situation forever," said Alfred.

"No, she reduces problems. It is all about the work. If you are causing problems and hindering her work process, *YOU* are a problem. It is really that simple. Just focus on the work. She appreciates people who work. Work is the key to everything for her. She will look over most flaws if you are working and making a strong effort. Look at the way she treats her students. Same deal. This is why they love her. She is direct. The students know the deal. Work, you will do well in her course."

"The students love you also," said Alfred.

"She trained me."

"I can make the effort. I just want to know that, at some point, I can get out of the doghouse," asserted Alfred.

"Good luck. It may take a long time. You should instead focus on the work. The rest will come."

"So, work," replied Alfred.

"Yes and stop trying to talk to her."

"Is there anything else that you think that I can do to make the project move forward?" requested Alfred.

"Can you start the mockup for the publication options and align it with the research methods?"

"Of course. I think that Petrot will be happy about this aspect. I know that she typically includes quantitative and qualitative methods in her articles," said Alfred.

"It increases the likelihood of a publication. Rot focuses on business. We must make sure that she sees the opportunities and *our* team."

"I do not want Marcus on the team. Pricilla informed me that Marcus is trying to take her spot," said Alfred, leaning back in the chair.

"When did she have time to tell you this?"

"She found me after one of my classes today," stated Alfred.

"Does Pricilla work? She has so much time to disseminate gossip."

Ignoring my comment, Alfred replied, "Pricilla has the higher degree of the two. No one respects Marcus. No one on campus calls him Dr. Pimpleton. This is a sign of respect. The student doesn't even respect him."

"They both have the highest degree within their discipline, and the students do respect him."

"Not President Miller," said Alfred.

"President Miller is cordial, but she respects very few people. You must serve a purpose to her."

Alfred responded back quickly by stating, "Marcus is on the student service side, and he has fewer publications. I do not think that he has had any publications in the last two years. This will have an impact on the ranking of our application, especially if Petrot insists that Bronston is not on the team."

"Removing Bronston is not an option. The team I assembled last night is the winning team."

"So, we agree about Marcus?" asked Alfred.

"Yes, but why the sudden push for Pricilla from you?"

"I notice things," stated Alfred.

"You noticed what?"

"You purposely have limited interactions with Marcus. This behavior began once you arrived on campus. I was in the front office when you were issued your ID. You stared at Marcus once he came into the office, but you said nothing. I initially thought you did not know each other," stated Alfred.

"I did not see you on my first day."

"I know, but I saw you. I typically blend into the background," declared Alfred.

"Really?"

"You often make an excuse to leave a designated location whenever the two of you are within arm's length at a university function. In some cases, you leave the room entirely," said Alfred.

"I have never said anything to you or *anyone* else about Marcus."

"Your demeanor changes in his presence. I noticed. I also noticed your interaction during the infamous holiday party. The conversation was low, but heated," articulated Alfred with a level of conviction.

"You did not say anything during that party."

"Sometimes it is good to be quiet. People underestimate silence. I notice things, and he makes your skin crawl. Even today, he came into Petrot's office, and you were out of her office in minutes," said Alfred.

"I thought you had already gone to your office."

"I did, but I walked back because I was going to confirm an aspect with the two of you before sending the email," expressed Alfred.

"What aspect?"

"The email location to send it. I did not know if we had a designated location for the team yet," said Alfred.

"Good save. Did you prepare this answer before walking back? I do not behave in this manner toward Marcus."

Ignoring a portion of my response, Alfred whispered, "I am not trying to make you feel uncomfortable, but why does he bother you? Is it something from graduate school?"

"We have known each other since graduate school, but he does not bother me."

"Okay. No need to elaborate. He is not going to be on *our team*. He serves no purpose and reduces our chance of winning the grant. It is a business decision," said Alfred.

I pulled a pen out of my seventeenth-century French Mazarin writing desk and scribbled on a notepad. I placed the pen within in his reach. I knew he would take it as a consolation prize. I did not want him to take my graduation pen.

Alfred took the pen off the desk and started to collect himself. I assumed that he was worried that I would request this pen back also. He hurried toward the door and looked back and said, "*Your* team from last night will be in place. I will make sure of it. I will find Petrot—no, email her to make sure that she needs nothing else presently."

"I would wait until tomorrow to email her."

"See, you are always looking out for me," said Alfred.

"I know you truly have a good heart."

"Trust me, Marcus will not be a worry of yours in a *few* days. I promise you that aspect. No one is going to bother you. I will not allow it. The team will be set because we need to get the rest of the project done, and Marcus is not going to create an uncomfortable environment for you anymore," replied Alfred.

I thought about correcting Alfred, but I knew that there was no point. He already had his mind made up about Marcus. As Alfred was leaving the office and turned to the right, Pricilla popped up in the door.

"Hi, Alfred, bye, Alfred. Have a great night," stated Pricilla. "Can you believe what happened at the hearing?"

"No. I have only heard rumors about the process and the protest. I also heard that the closing argument from Marie's side was strong. I figured, however, that they would make a decision quickly."

"I heard the protest changed the landscape of the situation, and President Miller is upset," expressed Pricilla, closing the door slightly.

"She has been upset since this morning, and the media crew did not help the situation."

"You know she hates bad publicity and the possibility of impacting the school's brand. Have you talked to Bronston yet?" asked Pricilla.

"No. He has other things on his plate, and he may not be looking for me."

"Yeah, right. Okay. I think his mother left campus about forty minutes ago," said Pricilla.

"Stop acting like you do not know the exact time that the woman departed from campus."

"I do not know the exact time, but I heard that she was very upset about the performance of their legal team and the protest by Ms. Walker," stated Pricilla.

"How do you know these aspects? Do you ever work?"

"I do work," stated Pricilla.

"When?"

"I had two classes today," stated Pricilla.

"Did you teach them, or did you have your graduate assistant cover those classes?"

"I made an appearance. The students needed to be in my glow for a moment. They needed to see my Chanel outfit. It is new," said Pricilla.

"Do you hear yourself?"

"What's the *real* problem? I am not the only person that provides an opportunity for my graduate students to gain teaching experience. Hello, Bronston," said Pricilla.

"*I* never said it was a problem."

"You know I am providing a valuable service," stated Pricilla, coming further into my office and taking a seat in one of my chairs.

"I got it, but you also realize that you must make more than an appearance. The students must always come first."

"This is the same argument that Petrot made to Bronston. I was there that day when a basic conversation turned into a brawl between the two of them. Not literally, of course. If I did not know better, I would swear that they dated at some point in graduate school," said Pricilla.

"They did not."

"If they did, you would never tell the truth. The relationship between the three of you is complicated to say the least. You are thicker than thieves, and the tide has only changed recently," stated Pricilla.

"Okay, let's tell a little truth."

"I am willing to play," stated Pricilla.

"You have been determined today to manipulate everything and make yourself present when your presence has not been requested."

"I have not."

"Think about it. This is the second time that I am seeing you today."

"We are friends, and I needed to update you," uttered Pricilla.

"We are, but I do not remember asking for the updates."

Pricilla looked hurt for a moment and squeaked out, "Wow."

"No, I have more truth."

"Please continue," whispered Pricilla.

"You found—and let me stress found—Alfred after class. How long did it take to look up his schedule? How long did you wait for him?"

"We bumped into each other," said Pricilla.

"For a man who you defined as always wearing clothing from the late 80s, I find that hard to believe that you bumped into him."

"Did you see his outfit today? It is from the 70s, but we honestly just bumped into each other. I needed to find him to provide him with updates," stated Pricilla.

"On what?"

"On the team," stated Pricilla.

"So, he is also your friend now?"

"He is my teammate," stated Pricilla.

"You have been bumping into a lot of people today. You had a horrible conversation with Rot last night, but you could not let it go."

"You suggested that I talk to her. Let's pause here for a moment. I know you did not tell me a secret about Rot. I mentioned it last night, and she did not flinch," asserted Pricilla.

"Rot never shows her cards."

"No, I knew you would never tell me anything of value against her, and she knows it also. Thank you for having me look like a fool in front of her," uttered Pricilla as she shook her head with a level of disdain.

"You cannot confirm this aspect. The key to a secret is keeping it. Maybe I was trying to see how long it would take for you to threaten her. If you cannot keep a secret for three days, maybe everyone is right for your level of involvement in anything."

Flailing her arms around and being very dramatic, Pricilla said, "I can keep a secret. I did not say it. I just stated that I knew a secret. The three of you are always playing games and never letting anyone truly into your group."

"Maybe the key was determining if you could follow directions. I specifically said not to threaten Petrot with the secret and only talk to her if it seemed appropriate. Did you listen? No."

"I thought I could help her see my side of the situation," said Pricilla.

"Exactly my point. You always feel like you are going to talk your way into everyone's good graces or on your side. And if that does not work, you threaten the person. Take a moment to listen and read the room."

Calming down a bit, Pricilla said, "Let me add a little truth to your reality."

"Please."

"Bronston, Petrot, and you are bullies that always get their way. The rest of us are just trying to be part of the club. You have the entire college within a groupthink framework. Individual faculty members are making poor choices, just so that they can belong to your elite club," said Pricilla.

"It seems like no one would want to be a part of the club or would ignore the groupthink process and think on their own."

"Yeah, right. Who would not want to be associated with the main three people on campus excelling and constantly helping each other? And let me stress again—the relationship just changed recently," said Pricilla.

"Wow, so I am assuming that this is your effort to get into the club. How is it working? Insulting people and threatening to tell their secrets is a quality that most people embrace."

"My interactions over the last twenty-four hours have not been the most productive," said Pricilla.

"Your secret could literally end your career, but you are insulting and threatening other people. Some of whom hold your secret."

"I do not think you realize how much stress I am under at this moment. People knowing my birth identity within the changing climate of the nation and state could result in several ramifications for me. I may not be totally on track for my objectives for today, but I have a goal," said Pricilla.

"The climate concerning sexual orientation and identity is changing."

"Tell that to the people presently living in Florida or Texas," said Pricilla.

"It is more so on the primary-school level."

"Yeah, right. Wake up," proclaimed Pricilla.

My computer changed color. It was a message from Bron stating to contact him once Pricilla was gone. How did he know she was in the office? Did he walk by and hear her voice?

"I know you are under a lot of pressure, but that does not give you the right to treat people poorly or to bother Rot."

"I bothered (your term) Alfred today also, but I notice that you only mentioned Petrot," said Pricilla.

"I mentioned Alfred. Shall I rewind today's tape for you?"

"No need, but I need Petrot on my side," affirmed Pricilla.

"Why? She is not the only lawyer in town."

Pricilla's voice got a little louder for emphasis, but not shouting, and said, "But she is the only lawyer that sleeps with the university handbook," said Pricilla.

"Any lawyer can learn that information."

"Yes, any lawyer can study it. But no one can touch Petrot concerning nuances of a policy," said Pricilla.

"You are correct. She has honed that skill."

"And you know she had something to do with the events that happened today. It was like watching a perfectly performed play," said Pricilla.

The computer screen changed color again. Bron was determined to talk to me but without Pricilla.

"She had nothing to do with today."

"I thought we were speaking the truth today," uttered Pricilla as she started to move again within the limited space within my office.

"Her involvement has not been confirmed."

"Every aspect on campus including the protest has aligned with her research and class lectures. This is a huge coincidence," said Pricilla, raising her eyes.

"I think you are mixing apples and oranges."

"I know that you will never go against either one of them. However, I do not think that you get it. I will do anything to be on this team and to remove Marcus. I never really liked him," said Pricilla, changing the subject.

"Is this today, or has this been festering for a long time concerning Marcus?"

Pricilla leaned closer to me and said, "I do not like the way that he looks at people. And I do not believe that he likes the three of you. He tolerates all three of you. Petrot cannot see it because he is constantly looking up her material for her publications. He is the type of person that wants his name on everything regardless of his contribution. This will not end if he is on the team. And who wants to deal with that? A person that does not contribute."

The computer screen changed color. It was Bron. My eyes shifted back to Pricilla.

"No one wants someone that will not contribute."

"And after talking to Alfred, I realized that we both do not like him," stated Pricilla.

"I am sensing that the two of you talked for longer than a moment."

"Not long," said Pricilla, shifting the conversation again, "If my secret comes out, we will not be able to make the mortgage payments. My only safeguard is to be associated with the team. This will hold me past the rumors and possible bad press. President Miller will ignore any problems if I have the backing of the team. Petrot will be able to talk me out of any situation."

"President Miller will always do what is in *her* best interest. This is a quality that you can count on, and Rot cannot solve everything."

"Yeah, right. The three of you bring distinctive traits to the table. You are strongest when you are together. I must admit—the team you gathered for the grant will have everything," said Pricilla.

"This is the strangest conversation that I have ever had with a person."

"Let me give you a few more truths. Marie knows she cannot win. The objective was to embarrass Bronston," said Pricilla.

"What?"

"Here are a few more aspects to consider. What if Marie is trying to get back at Petrot and Bronston?" asked Pricilla.

"What?"

"The best way to divide them is to focus on Petrot's passion. Hence my statement that they had a relationship in the past. What if Bronston refused an offer by Marie for a relationship? She may have assumed that Petrot was his goal, and they were more than friends. Once she got the refusal from Bronston, Petrot became her enemy. Obsession makes you do crazy things," said Pricilla.

"What?"

"Think about it. I will deny that I stated this portion. I never brought this to you to tell Bronston. I tell you everything. Maybe I did not tell you because Marie's statement did not make sense to me, and it did not sound like she was talking about a faculty member," articulated Pricilla.

"What?"

"Marie had been working with Petrot for over six months. She knows the procedure to make a claim, so why take so long to file?" asked Pricilla.

"Maybe she was trying to ignore the situation. This is a classic response, which has been found in academic research."

"Does Marie seem like a person that would ignore the situation or not take advantage of her resources?" asked Pricilla.

"You are stereotyping."

"Maybe but think about this. You had a hard time finding people who would vouch for Bronston because he is not very nice, but he is not that person," replied Pricilla.

"I know."

"Marie has worked for Bronston for a long time, and she is very aware of all his possible responses to a situation. I know she was upset about not being placed on his last grant even though it was small," said Pricilla.

"This does not add to the story, but it was not a small grant."

"Always protecting them both. Remember, she is a dual major, psychology and criminal justice, so she would have some tools in her arsenal to manipulate a situation," said Pricilla.

"Which you would recognize quickly."

"Maybe the situation got away from her once she signed the form, and she was forced now to play it out. Once it arrives to the Title IX coordinator, the office must investigate. Bronston was supposed to try to handle the situation quietly," articulated Pricilla.

"Mm."

"The case is taking longer than expected and not having the desired result from the protest today. Most people tell the truth to a close friend. Namely my teaching assistant," said Pricilla.

"What?"

Pricilla got up and stood at my door and said, "So let me state my worth again. I am going to do anything to be on the team. In a few days, Marcus will not be a problem. Tell Bronston to talk to Petrot. The three of you work the best together."

I emailed Bron that Pricilla was gone. He walked down immediately.

"I only have a minute. I must meet my mother. She is coming back to pick me up even though my car is in the parking lot. I know she will send the driver to pick my car up," said Bron.

"I have a lot to tell you."

"I just wanted you to hear it from me first. I am going to kill Rot. Our friendship ended once the protest started today," stated Bron, looking me squarely within my eyes.

"You both are misreading the situation, especially Rot."

Chapter Ten
Dr. Sarah Petrot

WEDNESDAY

It took me a moment to walk into the medieval building that held my office. Most universities had some building on campus that seemed out of place. This was our building. I had never been late for work, but I was forced to give the impression that my schedule changed due to a lunatic. I usually got up very early on Thursday and wrote before I went to the gym. After a light breakfast, I made my way to the research lab to ensure that the new projects were progressing at the designated weekly pace. This ensured that I was prepared for the weekend and had a balanced life. I enjoyed going to church and doing some type of physical exercise outside on the weekend. I would not partake in either of these items unless I was ahead of schedule, or I would be in the lab over the weekend. This formula had worked well since graduate school.

But last night, I tossed and turned because I received a note in my office. The conversation with Jo did not help. I had been receiving nicely wrapped packages for the last few days without a note. Unfortunately, I had to inform Lieutenant Alenzo of my packages because now I was getting notes. He was not happy that I had kept this information from him. I really did not want to make an issue about it. His lack of experience did not increase my level of assurance that something would happen under his watch, so I found no need to inform him of the packages. I just removed it from my office. I was usually the first person into the office, so I was able to discard any item and clean up. This was not the first time that a person responded in an unhealthy way to my win. The law office once had to hire a security detail for me over a three-week period until they caught the guy that was trying to kill me. The firm had no problem hiring the detail because I found a clause that protected our client, resulting in us winning the case and the client not having to pay millions to several people. Needless to say, the client was happy and offered me a job at his office. He called once a year to offer me a job. I declined his offer then and every time he called me. I found out some interesting aspects concerning the company that I would never be able to expose legally. The man was not wrapped properly.

The man who had made several attempts to kill me had been locked up for the last few years and would not be returning to society. I checked his status and whereabouts at the end of each month. I felt comfortable knowing that the state was still providing him with housing. This was why I was not a fan of changing my schedule to accommodate a *nut butter*. The person already had an insight into your routine. They typically had been following you before they made the first contact. The key was to get the person to show themselves and use *your* schedule to *your* advantage. Once law enforcement followed my advice concerning the law firm incident, we were able to catch the culprit. However, the entire incident resulted in me being open to Bron's offer to look at Mill Run. Anyone could get into any office on campus once the building opened. The office suites did not have any type of alarm system or updated lock system.

The note on my desk was *like* a cult movie classic. The note said, "I know what you did in your past." This was like the movie, *I Know What You Did Last Summer*. This was the first note. However, over the last few days, I had been receiving some type of animal blood in a jar. The smell was always a warm welcome upon my arrival. Yesterday, it was pig's blood. I did appreciate the fact that it always had a teal ribbon on it to make it look like a gift. The spin on horror movies was also a nice touch in the note. Everyone knew I loved horror movies. After receiving my note, Lieutenant Alenzo was adamant about making sure that he arrived at my office before I arrived and monitored my office space once I departed for the day.

I had no intention of allowing anyone to enter my office before I arrived there. I got to my office close to two hours earlier than my scheduled time. I used the overnight system. I had to use my university ID card to enter the building, but I knew the amateurish lieutenant would not realize for a few days that I had come into the building early on this date. The office suite was quiet, and there was nothing on my desk upon my arrival. This confirmed that the person was not entering my office space before the building had officially opened. Jo had informed me last night that Bron was gearing up to kill me. I was so frightened as I expressed my concern to her by laughing. She did not think that I was funny.

She stated that we all needed to talk before the grant meeting. I had no intention of going to the grant meeting tonight because nothing had been decided concerning Bron. The president had stopped the process because of the protest. I knew she had really stopped the process because the committee had not determined a verdict quickly, and she was trying to figure out a way to neutralize the situation. The real objective was for her to come out on top. I also knew based on the continuance of the hearing that Bron did not take her offer. To my surprise, I heard both Jonathan and the lieutenant talking at my front door after I had been in the office for an hour. The building had just officially opened.

"What are *you* doing here?" asked Lieutenant Alenzo.

"I came to place some material on Dr. Petrot's door. What are *you* doing here?" asked Jonathan.

"I am just checking out the building," stated Lieutenant Alenzo.

"And a specific location in the building?" asked Jonathan.

"Stop acting like you don't know what happened yesterday,," replied Lieutenant Alenzo.

"I have no idea of what you are talking about. If you are looking for Dr. Petrot, I would assume that she is up in the research lab by now *if* she is in the building early. She always checks the status of her projects before making decisions about her week and weekend," said Jonathan.

"How do you know *all* this information about her?" asked Lieutenant Alenzo.

"I *work* for her. What happened yesterday? Is Dr. Petrot okay?" asked Jonathan with a hint of concern in his voice.

"Oh, I guess she does not tell you everything," said Lieutenant Alenzo.

"Please just tell me what happened, Dad," responded Jonathan, raising his voice but being respectful.

"Do not raise your voice at me," stated Lieutenant Alenzo.

"Yes, sir," replied Jonathan.

"Talking back to me is not an option. I did not say anything in front of Dr. Petrot the other night because I did not want to embarrass you," stated Lieutenant Alenzo.

"Yes, sir," replied Jonathan.

"Not that I should be telling you this, but her stalker has escalated the situation," said Lieutenant Alenzo.

"How?" asked Jonathan.

"The stalker placed a note on her desk. Did you know that she has been getting packages over the last few days?" asked Lieutenant Alenzo.

"No," stated Jonathan.

"Are you sure?" asked Lieutenant Alenzo.

"No. I did not know that she was receiving wrapped packages," said Jonathan.

"I did not say that the items were wrapped," said Lieutenant Alenzo.

"Most packages are wrapped. You sound a little paranoid," stated Jonathan.

"I honestly do not recognize you. I think you are lying now. You know that she has been having a problem. This is why you are here now; you are trying to catch the person," stated Lieutenant Alenzo.

"I am not trying to catch someone," stated Jonathan.

"Yes, you are. The building just opened. YOU are trying to catch the culprit. You know her schedule. *YOU* know when there are gaps," said Lieutenant Alenzo.

"No, I am dropping off information for the next paper. I talk about our work all the time at home. This is not a new behavior. We are always working on something. Hence I will always be dropping off something," stated Jonathan.

"Yeah, right," expressed Lieutenant Alenzo.

"Why would you say something like that to me?" asked Jonathan.

"You are always with her," asserted Lieutenant Alenzo.

"I'm not a child. I am getting sick of people questioning our relationship. This would not be happening if she was a man. No one would have a problem with our working relationship," continued Jonathan.

"Gender has nothing to do with it," uttered Lieutenant Alenzo.

"Gender has everything to do with it, and you have never looked at me beyond being a QB. You cannot fathom that I have anything to offer anyone intellectually," expressed Jonathan.

"Being a QB was your golden ticket," said Lieutenant Alenzo.

"Regardless of if I still loved the sport or not," articulated Jonathan.

"You love football," stated Lieutenant Alenzo.

"You love it. Let me give you some food for thought. Last week, based on my research, she got me a working gig," stated Jonathan.

"What kind of *gig*?" asked Lieutenant Alenzo.

"She got me a speaking engagement at a prominent women's organization. I presented on sexual misconduct from a male perspective. She showed me how to brand myself to that market," said Jonathan.

"It was probably for free," stated Lieutenant Alenzo with an air of confidence.

"No. She taught me to never give anything away for free unless it enhances my overall goal," said Jonathan.

"Really?" asked Lieutenant Alenzo.

"Really. The organization paid me $1,500 for three hours of work at my level. It was one hour for the presentation and two hours for preparation and travel," said Jonathan.

"I cannot believe that," stated Lieutenant Alenzo.

"Believe it. Just think, I am doing this at an undergraduate level," said Jonathan.

"Well, she is also getting you involved in this protest. She is not thinking about your career in that situation," said Lieutenant Alenzo, trying to prove a point.

"Pardon me?" stated Jonathan.

"You heard me. You were either the hoodie person or the person at the library yesterday. You know everyone on campus, and everyone would help you get away," said Lieutenant Alenzo.

"I did not participate in the incident yesterday, and you cannot prove anything," answered Jonathan.

"What the heck? I am your father, and why would I need to prove anything?" asked Lieutenant Alenzo.

"I am telling you that I had nothing to do with the protest. You refuse to believe me. I have never lied to you," said Jonathan.

"But you are quite aware of how to manipulate a conversation and hedge the truth. I must admit that she is teaching you a lot of new tricks. I am telling you that I have not recognized you ever since you quit the football team," stated Lieutenant Alenzo.

"Now the truth comes out. We are back to this conversation?" asked Jonathan.

"We never really had it," stated Lieutenant Alenzo, getting louder.

"Or is the real issue that you cannot let something go or stop controlling my life? You refuse to let me live my life. Football was an option that I explored, and now I am going in a new direction," said Jonathan.

"Football gave you options," stated Lieutenant Alenzo.

"Football was one option. I have new options. This is exactly why I am moving into my own apartment in two months. I will be able to afford it," said Jonathan, talking lower to encourage his father to lower his voice.

"Just because she got you *one* speaking engagement does not mean that you will be able to afford rent," stated Lieutenant Alenzo.

"I have another one next month, but I also have a job," said Jonathan.

"The school position is not going to cover everything," said Lieutenant Alenzo with assurance.

"I have more than one job. I wait tables on the weekends. I work the grave shift. Drunk people love me. And women love having the school's retired QB wait on them. I have 'regulars' waiting until I come on my shift. I play into their fantasy," said Jonathan.

"I thought you discouraged men taking advantage of women," stated Lieutenant Alenzo.

"I am not taking advantage of anyone, and I talk about consent the entire time. Dr. Petrot showed me how to respect women, but I must pay my bills. I cannot help it if I work out every day and stay in shape. I also cannot help it if they enjoy tapping me on the butt and leaving me a huge tip," said Jonathan, laughing a bit.

"I thought you were hanging out with friends," said Lieutenant Alenzo with a level of disappointment in his voice.

"No, sir. I am making an investment in my life. I make sure that I balance my time. I only work the second job on the weekend because Dr. Petrot will place me on the curb if I miss any dates," stated Jonathan.

Oh, he *was* listening to me. I would kick him to the curb if his grades dipped in any fashion or if the publications interfered with his work.

"This woman controls your life," declared Lieutenant Alenzo.

"No. You are overthinking the situation. She has taught me how to advance quickly. I am ahead of schedule concerning my funds. This short, focused effort on my part will put me on a distinctive path," articulated Jonathan.

"No, moving out is still up for discussion between your mother and I," replied Lieutenant Alenzo.

"Perfect example. I am a grown man that will be turning twenty-one soon. It is my decision, not your decision. I have the money. I can support myself," pronounced Jonathan.

"We still give you money," answered Lieutenant Alenzo.

"No, ask Mom. I stop taking money from you a year ago," articulated Jonathan.

"Once you started working for her," stated Lieutenant Alenzo.

"This situation is between you and me. Dr. Petrot has nothing to do with it. I also do not appreciate that you found out yesterday about her situation, and you mentioned nothing about it at dinner. If it was any other person, you would have mentioned it at dinner without hesitation," said Jonathan.

"I assumed you knew what was going on, and I did not want to mention it to everyone in the family," said Lieutenant Alenzo.

"Believe whatever you want, but you know that statement was not true," said Jonathan, getting a bit louder.

"It is true," stated Lieutenant Alenzo, raising his voice.

"Okay. You mention Dr. Petrot at every meal. I should have known something was off when you only mentioned her once. My mistake. I assumed that you had finally moved on," stated Jonathan, raising his voice a bit more.

"Not every meal," uttered Lieutenant Alenzo, getting louder.

"Yes, you do. You just do not realize it," stated Jonathan, matching his tone.

I realized that this was my opportunity to make noise, so that I could emerge from my office. I felt like they both would assume that they missed my entrance in the back door, and I emerged at the front door.

"Hello, gentlemen."

"Are you okay?" asked Jonathan, seriously concerned.

"I am fine. Why wouldn't I be fine?"

Jonathan knew that his father was *not* supposed to mention any problems concerning my office yesterday or over the last few days. Everyone was aware that I had a stalker, but he should not know the details unless they came from me. I wanted to see if he knew not to say anything.

Jonathan articulated quickly, "You are here thirty minutes before your usual window of arrival or during this time you are usually in the lab. I thought something might be wrong with the submission."

"No, we are set. Lieutenant Alenzo, your son is such a perfectionist. Has he always been this way?"

"He seems to be learning new tricks every day," stated Lieutenant Alenzo, staring at his son.

"One day I will beat you to the office," stated Jonathan, trying to change the subject.

"I thought you were coming into the office later," stated Lieutenant Alenzo, confirming that I had adjusted his assigned schedule for me.

"And a good morning to you too, Lieutenant Alenzo. I forgot that I needed to get some work done before your son arrived this morning. I wanted to make sure that I did not get behind schedule. He runs a tight ship."

Jonathan quietly smirked.

"I, however, need to get to the research lab soon. Did you need me for anything, or were you just doing a routine walk through the building?"

"Routine," uttered Lieutenant Alenzo.

Lieutenant Alenzo knew to make it seem like he was just walking through the building in front of Jonathan. I did not look in his direction, but I could feel Jonathan smiling.

"Are you all set?" asked Lieutenant Alenzo, not alluding to my situation.

"I am, but the day is young. I realize now that only certain people can get into the building once it is unlocked."

"Yes. I guess *someone* was right about that aspect," stated Lieutenant Alenzo, staring at me for a bit.

I got the feeling that he hated it when I was correct about anything. I really did not understand why.

"The building must be open for anyone to start wandering into various sections regardless of if the cleaning crew is in the building," uttered Lieutenant Alenzo.

"It seems to narrow down certain options for a *person*."

Trying to ignore my points, Lieutenant Alenzo shifted the conversation and stated, "I will see you later in the morning. I am not sure if you got the email, but President Miller has moved the meeting until 11 a.m. She must meet with the board before she talks to the two of us."

Okay, this fool had crossed a line. I had no intention of telling anyone about my relationship with President Miller. I was also assuming that dissemination of my relationship by him had not only been told to Jonathan but anyone else that would listen to him. This was why you kept your main circle of associates small and concise. Thus, I smiled with a smirk and said, "Looking forward to seeing you at 11. I will be coming from my class."

"I know. She checked to make sure that you were free. Have a good morning," said Lieutenant Alenzo.

I quickly turned back to Jonathan and gave him a huge smile, raising one eyebrow, and asked, "Now why are you *really* here so early?"

"I looked up some material," answered Jonathan.

"Okay, let me see."

"I have a question," stated Jonathan.

"What's up?"

"How much of that conversation did you hear?" asked Jonathan.

"Do you really want to know?"

"No. I am embarrassed that this is the third time this week someone has questioned our relationship. People are treating me like a dumb jock, and I am incapable of existing in an intellectual environment. I have so much to offer," whispered Jonathan.

"I know that. I told you that."

This was a really big issue for him. It took me a couple of weeks to convince him that he could do it and be competitive in the academic arena. He was killing it in everything and handling his schedule.

"You are the only person that looks at me with educational aspirations that I can do this," said Jonathan, looking down.

"Look up. You only need one person." I waited until Jonathan raised his head. "Remember, I amount to having a crowd on your side."

"I know. I would do anything for you. I would never let anyone hurt you. You would never have to ask me to protect you. I would analyze the situation and take care of it," stated Jonathan.

"I know you are worried about the stalker, but I will be fine. This is not the first time and unfortunately will not be the last time that I have a problem with a person. You are not supposed to worry about me. I am supposed to worry about you. I am older."

"You have done everything for me. No one is ever going to hurt you on my watch," said Jonathan.

"Let's focus on the work and not my safety. I woke up feeling fine. I would like to stay on that path."

We walked into my office. Jonathan went to his table, and I went to my desk.

"So, I found this article that I think will clear up the point that you are trying to make," said Jonathan, handing me the article.

"It sounds like the student is becoming the master in this publication."

"You know that I want this to be my area of concentration," said Jonathan.

We worked on the material extensively for the next hour and half. This interrupted my research lab time. I felt out of sorts. I had a feeling that the day was going to be interesting.

"Oh, I need to get ready for class and so do you, so get out."

Laughing, Jonathan packed up his items and whispered, "Thank you for everything."

"Keep on sounding crazy. I will drop you like a hot potato."

"You know you can pick a potato up and brush it off," stated Jonathan.

"So, we have jokes today."

"I figured that I should step up my game," laughed Jonathan.

"Oh Lord. Bye."

"See you later this afternoon?" asked Jonathan.

"Check your email. I may have other obligations."

"Okay, but we have not fully outlined the schedule for the next paper," said Jonathan.

"Such a taskmaster. Bye."

"Bye," said Jonathan, finally leaving the office.

"Good morning, Jonathan," said Pricilla. Her voice made me cringe. I could only imagine what she wanted now. It was like she was a whack-a-mole. I kept hitting her down, and she kept popping up.

"Good morning, Dr. Appleton. Have a nice day, Dr. Petrot. I will see you later," said Jonathan.

"Do not forget to check your email!"

After Jonathan was out of earshot, Pricilla said, "It took him a minute to leave."

"What do you want? Why are you even in the building today? You do not teach today."

"You know we use to have wonderful conversations," stated Pricilla.

"When we were friends."

"Why is everything a black or white situation for you?" asked Pricilla.

"I actually *love* the gray, but this is not the first time that I have forgiven you. It was not so long ago when you accused me of trying to take your family."

After Bron *pushed* Pricilla down the stairs, my aunt and I moved into her home and helped her family. She had a lot of issues and was very dramatic to say the least. The family schedule was horrible. They did not have a schedule. I could not take it. It was driving me crazy, and my aunt knew I was going to crack after a few hours. The schedule changed after one night. Let's say that I could be charismatic when the need arose.

Her family complained at the beginning, but then everyone fell into line. It helped tremendously that my aunt made all the meals, including lunch for everyone. Food could convince people to do many things. I was trying to eat healthy, so everyone had to go with my meal choices, even Pricilla. The food was actually really good even though it was healthy. I kept telling my aunt to write a book.

We had dinner at 6:00 p.m. every night. Pricilla had no choice in the matter because she really could not move. During the first two weeks of the Spring term, Pricilla taught her classes over Zoom. This was fine because students were used to this structure due to COVID. She did, however, hire a makeup artist to do her hair and makeup before each session. She informed me that she had an image to maintain, and neither I nor her partner had the skillset to help her. For the rest of the month, we figured out how to maintain both our schedules, and Pricilla's partner applied for a promotion., We celebrated the promotion the next month. Pricilla and I also got three publications out of the situation. One was with Jo. I figured that we should maximize our time.

I got really close to her two children, but especially her daughter. She was preparing for the spelling bee. We went over words constantly, and she studied with my aunt when I was not there. She even called me at the office a couple of times. Of course, I took her call. She never went to bed without meeting our daily amount of words. Needless to say, she won the local competitions with ease. On the day of the national competition, we had to drive to a remote, small-town location in the state. We left Pricilla on the day of the competition because she was taking too long to get dressed for the program. She could not figure out what to wear to the event. She kept asking whether it was formal-casual or casual-formal. I did not understand the difference and ignored her. I was focused on the time.

"I told you that I had a reaction from my medication that night," expressed Pricilla.

"It was not a reaction. You were upset, and on the night of your daughter's special evening. It was embarrassing."

"I was just so hurt that she went to hug you first, and so did my partner," said Pricilla.

"We practiced together. This is why she went to me first. You should frame it like going to your coach first. And on top of it, we all did not know that you had arrived at the venue. You were in the back."

"I know. I just felt like it was not my night. I got there late, and no one was paying attention to me," said Pricilla.

"It was not *your* night or the night for you to get the perfect outfit. It was not about you."

"My family loves both you and your aunt. I tried to change the schedule again this month, and they refuse to do it. They said that they are more productive on the schedule. I feel like I am not included sometimes. We used to work for hours on a paper. This is why we got so much done. I have never worked so hard in my life," said Pricilla.

"I have nothing to do with your work production *OR* what's going on at your house now."

"I know my partner calls and gives you updates," stated Pricilla.

"I keep telling you that I am not in that situation."

"You have no idea of how it feels to be replaced," said Pricilla.

"I am not replacing you. I was helping you."

"I know. I just want to be a part of all components of my life. My family structure is changing, and my friends are changing," stated Pricilla.

"My family shuffled you around for an entire month, and the thanks you gave me was accusing me of taking your family. Even now, you are trying to blame me for your current situation."

"I am not blaming you," said Pricilla.

"You're right. You are playing the victim card."

With her arms flailing around and being very dramatic, Pricilla said, "No. I am trying to show you that I can be a *great* team player. I know you have a long day ahead because you are helping Bronston. Do you need me to prepare anything for you?"

"Teaching is not your lane. You are a five out of ten at best. So, I am assuming that you are trying to confirm your *tea* today?"

"No, I am trying to help. I can play a video or something in one of his classes. I am also trying to confirm that I will see you sometime today to talk, *OR* I will stalk you until you give me the focused time. I want to talk to you before the meeting tonight," said Pricilla.

"I never said I was going to the team meeting."

"You never said that you would not go," declared Pricilla.

"I stormed out of the room that night. This would signal *to me* that I was not coming back. So again, I am assuming that you are confirming your *tea*?"

"You know I do more things than gossip," stated Pricilla.

"Really?"

"So, am I another *stalker* on your list today, or would you like to place me on the schedule? You know, pencil me in. And yes, I am aware of all your locations today. It was a matter of looking you up and crossing Bronston's schedule. It only took a few minutes. I do not think people realize how easy it is to stalk a professor or anyone on campus," said Pricilla.

"This provides me with great comfort. The ease with which you can locate my schedule and stalk me."

"I am providing you with an option. I know you appreciate a good option," said Pricilla.

"I appreciate being ignored."

"Sure, you do. People are required to listen to you talk at least three times a week. This screams a person that wants to be ignored," stated Pricilla.

"Part of my job is to lecture. Unlike you, I am not looking for a chance to perform or to have a SRTE at a five out of ten."

My computer changed color. It was a note from Bron that said, "I am going to kill you."

This guy never quit. I wondered if he was in the building or driving into the office when he sent this note. I knew his mother made him sleep at home last night. He was such a mom's boy. I turned my attention back to Pricilla. She seemed perturbed when I looked at my screen.

"Tell yourself whatever you would like, but please do not feed me the line about wanting to be ignored. So, I guess I will see you either between this class and your meeting with the president or after your meeting. I may walk with you to your meeting. And yes, everyone knows you have a meeting with President Miller at 11," said Pricilla.

"I must go to class, but what do you want to talk about during this meeting? Let me be clear. I am not going to the team meeting tonight."

"I want to talk to you about a few things," articulated Pricilla.

"You already said that statement. Talk now. I doubt it will last more than a few minutes."

Pricilla leaned forward and forcefully stated, "NO, I want to just want to sit down and talk. I want your focused attention and not your brush-me-off attention."

"So, we are going the yelling route. How did that work the *other* night?"

"Look. You can be so hurtful when you determine the person is not a friend or you are done."

"I am not being disrespectful to you. In fact, I am being pleasant. You are just not getting what you want, so you are acting like a child."

"I am not acting like a child."

"Really?"

"You know, words hurt," replied Pricilla.

"You should know, Ms. Psychology Major."

"Look, we are already going in the wrong direction."

"Again, what do you want?"

"I want to talk to you," pronounced Pricilla, and she noticed me looking at my watch and then to my computer screen.

"I guess you are required to teach my classes today. You're welcome! I also told Dr. Peaboy that you will be his replacement next term. He was quite surprised to hear the news. You're welcome," said Bron.

I wanted to respond to the email, but Pricilla was in the room. It was like Bron knew that she was in the room.

"We are talking now, Pricilla, and you have wasted about two and half minutes. I must go to class."

"I want to talk in a calm manner," articulated Pricilla.

"Then you are not going to be a part of this meeting?"

Pricilla stared at me for a moment, took a breath, and said, "I would like to request your presence to talk."

"Wow, the couple therapy sessions are working. Take one more breath. I would like to see this side of you again."

Pricilla took the breath and said, "I hate that I told you about them."

"You did not tell me about your therapy sessions. I found out about them when you were sick, and I helped take care of you. Boy, you love to rewrite history. Do you ever spill tea correctly?"

Pricilla ignored my response totally and stated, "Would I be able to fit into your schedule after your meeting with President Miller?"

"I am getting the feeling that talking to you later is not an option but a demand. I also get the feeling that you are not going to take no for an answer."

"No," said Pricilla.

"The day has already started out long, but I am happy that I got some research work done. Let's go with the stalker route."

"What?" asked Pricilla.

"I had an option. I am making the choice to add you to my list of stalkers. I am enjoying the breathing demonstrations by you. I would like to see how the day is going to work out with you. Let's make some rules concerning today."

"What?"

"Do not bump into me. I see no reason for you to touch me. We passed COVID season, but why increase my exposure, and why do you constantly find the need to be close to people when you are talking? You tend to be on top of a person when you talk and touch them."

"This is not true," uttered Pricilla.

"It is true. If you must use your calming-down method, the total amount of time I talk to you decreases by half. This should reduce my responsibility of talking to you entirely before our official designated time."

"So, you are going to give me time?" asked Pricilla.

"No, you are a stalker. People run from stalkers. You must catch me."

"I am not going to play your stupid game," stated Pricilla.

"You will play it. You cannot help yourself. You enjoy the competition. I just tapped into this aspect of your personality. You also want to prove to me that you can control yourself. But before you go, how did you know about my meeting with the president? The university has only been open for a few hours."

"You assume that I am not friends with people in the president's office," said Pricilla.

"You mean your gossip buddies. I forgot that you have a spy in every office. It is a wonder that you produce any publications."

"Do not forget that they are in the top journals of my discipline," declared Pricilla.

"I stand corrected. Publications in the top journal. And if I am not mistaken, two of your top-journal publications were with me."

Trying to stand her ground and gain some momentum, Pricilla stated, "I have others without you. Recognize that you are standing in front of greatness in my field unlike Marcus. Very few people make it to the top journals."

"No, and if I am not mistaken, I was one of the first few people to congratulate you on your solo publications. I also need to give you credit. It took you a minute before mentioning Marcus."

"What does he bring to any team?" asked Pricilla.

"Silence."

"You are a person that takes chances and hedges her bets. Marcus must add something else for you. You would swallow your pride if I served a purpose for you. Have you talked to Jo yet?" asked Pricilla.

"I cannot confirm or deny that I talked to Jo, and why would I tell you?"

Looking a little hurt but trying to make every effort to hide it, Pricilla overlooked this comment and went back to her conversation. "You need to talk to Jo. This whole situation with Bronston seems off. You are stronger together."

"Since when did you start caring about the three of us?"

"We are a team," stated Pricilla.

"We?"

Quickly shifting the conversation again, Pricilla said, "Look, this is why I want to talk to you later. The people in the president's office and everywhere else are not spies but my friends," declared Pricilla.

"I wonder how those friends will respond once they find out about the true you."

"This is exactly why I want to talk to you for more than a moment. I have a lot riding on this grant," uttered Pricilla.

"Look, I never go back on my promises. No one will ever hear about your secret from me."

"You know that it is more than just the secret, but the dwindling of my options once administration finds out," said Pricilla.

"You have options, but I am not going to help you. We are done."

"You know that I can be a potato that you pick up and brush off too," said Pricilla.

"Wow, so I know how long you were standing at the door."

"I just wanted you to realize that we used to joke around also," stated Pricilla.

"Not anymore. Okay. I must go. Unlike you, I do not like to be late."

"Fine. I will see you later," stated Pricilla.

"If you can catch me."

Chapter Eleven
Dr. Bronston Everstone

The university was situated on top of a hill. In order to reach the destination, you had to drive up a long, steep, distorted road. Unfortunately, many students had accidents on this road in an attempt to make it to campus quickly. My preference was not to drive to work, but today, I needed a moment alone. Jo had to be getting ready to teach class, but I needed to talk to her now. I took a chance and called her on her private line.

"Where are you? I hear an echo. Do you have me on speakerphone in your home office?" asked Jo.

"I know you are not a fan, but I am talking to you from my car phone."

"Why?" asked Jo.

"I am on my way to campus."

"Alone or with the driver?" asked Jo. I thought she could hear me shifting gears. I had a feeling she was making fun of me.

"I am driving myself."

"Stop acting like you do not have a driver on occasion. You are going to ruin that clutch. Take the time to shift correctly," said Jo.

"So, you answered the phone to yell at me."

"No, but that car cost more than some people's homes. Please take the time to shift correctly," declared Jo.

"I am. On another note, please do not hang up without saying goodbye. This has been a running theme for me over the last few days."

"What are you talking about?" asked Jo.

"Never mind."

"I just wanted to make sure that you are alone. I really do not want to say much over the phone, but Rot got a message on her desk yesterday," said Jo.

"Is the stalker situation escalating? Did he try to kill her yesterday? Is she dead?"

"No," stated Jo.

"He is *not* really a good stalker. She should be dead by now. I have been bothering her all morning. I knew she would be working with students this morning, and she could only see the messages from me and not respond. I informed her that I joined the list to kill her."

Lowering her voice, a bit—I guess I should have found out her location—she said, "Well she caught something on her camera in her office."

"What camera?"

"Really, we are going to play this game?" asked Jo.

"Okay, so I am not surprised that she has cameras in her office. What policy does that fall under?"

"She has not gotten caught yet. She has already prepared a statement on why and how *she* can have cameras in her office," said Jo, laughing.

"Naturally, she does."

"Any location in which she has authority has a camera system. Home, school, research lab, et cetera. You are not going to walk up on her," stated Jo, still laughing.

"It probably started after the incident at the law firm."

"I would assume, but I would not be surprised if it started in graduate school. She was very particular about keeping our work separate from others," said Jo.

Jo was right. Rot kept our work in a separate filing cabinet and in a separate encrypted file. I once forgot the password, and she would not let me enter the system for an entire month. A month. I had to ask permission to open the file. I had never forgotten a password since that date. I was honestly not sure if it was a conscious behavior or a subconscious behavior.

"Why is this of interest to me?"

"Well, she had a very interesting visitor yesterday," stated Jo.

"Who? I know she is not saying that I trashed her office."

"No. Focus," said Jo with emphasis.

"Then who?"

"Marcus," said Jo, whispering. I assumed that someone must have come close to her.

"What?"

"You heard me," said Jo.

"Why was he in her office? Did he trash it?"

"No. He left a note. He got the administrative assistant to open the door for him on the pretense that he had to leave research work for her. He has been working for her for the past year. She had no reason to doubt him," stated Jo.

"Yes, she did. Rot lets no one in her office. She has a list of ten rules that you do not break. She got someone fired in her first week at the school. The girl went home crying and never came back. She did not feel a drop of guilt about it. Everyone knows this rule. Jonathan waits for her. Outside of her door. No one has an extra set of keys. Do you?"

"No," said Jo.

"Not even in a case of an emergency."

"I told you no. No," said Jo, with accent.

"Why?"

"Because Security can let me into the office. She will make that call," said Jo.

"I think you have a key, and you're just not telling me. The administrative assistant is done."

"Get this—you can hear the entire conversation. He thanked her and everything for opening the door. She giggled and said no problem," stated Jo.

"She is really going to get it now. This guy is full of surprises. Never wants to do his own work."

"Are you really talking about doing your own work? Please do not tell me that you are not talking at this moment," said Jo.

"I delegate. There is a difference. So, what did the note say?"

"It was a play on a horror movie," said Jo.

"Which one?"

"*I Know What You Did Last Summer*," replied Jo.

"It is one of Rot's favorite movies."

"I know," whispered Jo. I started to wonder whether Jo was in the office or at home because she kept whispering at certain times.

"What did it say?"

"I know what you did in your past," stated Jo.

"How?"

"This is where the story gets interesting. Rot stated that he looked at a picture in her office of the three of us. The picture of us right after graduation with the Franklin quote engraved in the frame."

"She still has that picture? I would have thought it would be in the garbage after last week."

"She never has it out, so it was out by chance. She said Marcus looked at it, and then he had some type of revelation," said Jo.

"Of what?"

Jo coughed and said, "She said she had no idea."

"It sounds like a problem."

"She thought so also," said Jo.

"I guess I should not have threatened her life this morning. Is she willing to talk to me? It sounds like we have a collective problem."

"Well, we also talked about the Marie situation. I know you do not want to hear this, and neither did she, but I got the information from Pricilla concerning Marie," said Jo.

"Gossip queen."

"Yes, but I think she may have something. We are stronger together," said Jo.

"Rot said she needed to see Marie's statement. Your lawyer would have this information," stated Jo.

"What does she think is in the statement?"

"Marie knows your movements, but Rot had you down to a science during graduate school. She also sizes up *everyone* at her job. She takes the first full month to recognize and know everyone's idiosyncrasies. Marie's statement will help her determine the flaw in the story and where it falls apart. There are certain things that you just do not do," articulated Jo.

"I hate to admit it, but this is why the law firm wants her back."

"Yes. She loves finding a problem in a statement and then tripping up a person with their own words. You know that one of the partners from her old firm came to see last week. He just showed up after her last class. He looked up her schedule," said Jo.

"Is she leaving?"

"Do not get excited, but I honestly cannot tell. He sweetened the pot, and not a little bit," stated Jo.

"Rot has a plan. I am just not sure if the law firm fits in her plan. Why didn't you call me last night? I feel like I am missing out."

"You could barely talk to me yesterday. I had the feeling that you were on lockdown and had to get permission to talk on the phone from your mom," laughed Jo.

"Stop laughing at me. You and Rot act like you do not have family obligations. Rot to her aunt and you to your husband. Hi, pot, meet kettle."

"Good try, but your relationship with your mom is 'interesting.' I am not mad at it, but it is interesting," said Jo.

"You are right, but it works for us."

"Not all the time," said Jo.

"I am not going to open that graduate-school issue. So, is Rot open to all of us talking?"

"She is hurt that you would not follow her. You know that she is totally not to be blamed for *your* situation. Marie has been working with Rot, but I have a feeling that someone else has been feeding Marie information," said Jo.

"Who?"

"I think it may be Jonathan," stated Jo.

"Her shadow. I hate that guy."

"I think his hate for you is mutual. I really think he may be doing it to protect Rot. He is obsessed with her," proclaimed Jo.

"He is obsessed, but he is not crazy."

"I am not sure about that aspect. You have not seen the way that he looks at her," said Jo.

"It is just an infatuation. People are attracted to her mind."

"Sounds like you're talking from experience," said Jo, still laughing.

"Don't bring up graduate-school issues."

"Anyway. You made the choice to bring in your legal team. Rot told you to go and talk to the president first. She warned you of the steps that would follow. The president had to follow the Title IX procedure," stated Jo.

"I know, but Rot has been arguing with me for months now."

"You know that the two of you are always arguing about something else. This situation just gives you both an excuse to have an exchange even if the context is weird," said Jo.

"This is untrue."

"I wish the two of you would just stop. And on another note, why haven't you involved your mother more than a little? Rot made that suggestion also," stated Jo.

"Through you."

"How else was she to get the information to you? Your family has pull in the community on several different levels. You have never used it in the past, but this would be the time to use it," declared Jo.

"I didn't want to."

"No, you did not want to do it because you knew that Rot would be right. You hate following a woman, especially around your fraternity brothers," said Jo.

"This is not true."

"It is true. I am not sure if coming home was the best path for you. Your image here is different than in graduate school," said Jo.

"It is the same."

"No, it is different. You are trying to impress everyone at the country club. You do realize that you are cutting off your spoils of the earth. What's going to happen if you follow a woman? You will be happy. You follow your mother," said Jo.

"I am really afraid of her."

"We know. Tell me something new. You always realized your lane. You now want to own all the lanes, and you're not even willing to share. You only must share a bit with Rot. She has earned it," stated Jo.

"I know."

"This is why we did not call you last night," said Jo.

"You were afraid of what I would say."

"You think," said Jo.

"Where do we *all* stand now?"

"Marcus is the common enemy. We need to talk in person to deal with Marcus," said Jo.

"When?"

"After the meeting. We can take care of him then," whispered Jo and hung up.

I specifically requested that she not hang up without saying good-bye. Maybe she had to hang up because the person she was trying to avoid came back into the room. What was going on with all the women within my life? I just *needed* Rot to yell at me in person now, and my day would be set.

Chapter Twelve
Dr. Sarah Petrot

Mill Run had the hustle and bustle of students going from one class to another. Pricilla was correct. I had a long day of classes due to Peaboy. I had to cover my classes, and I also had to cover Bronston's classes, which it sounded like he was enjoying. I wondered why Peaboy had not strongly encouraged Marie to cover Bronston's classes. She had been doing them for a long time. I finally made it to my class with only three minutes to spare. Of course, a student had to declare to the class that I was running late.

"I am not running late."

The student informed me with confirmation from his cohorts that I always arrived seven to eight minutes before the start of class, in which I usually started the lecture. The only thing that I could do at that point was laugh. After the lecture, I walked out of the classroom with a few students surrounding me talking about some key points, but I ran straight into Pricilla.

"Tag, you're it," articulated Pricilla.

"Wow. I guess the hint to leave me alone went on deaf ears."

"Did you say to leave you alone, or did you say that this was a challenge?" questioned Pricilla.

"Touché."

Trying to keep a positive vibe, Pricilla said, "See, we can have fun."

"I only have a few minutes to drop off my bag and make it to the president's office."

"I know," confirmed Pricilla.

"Walk and talk."

"This is not our talking session. This is our banter session," declared Pricilla.

We rounded the corner to make it to my office, quickly passing several students as they acknowledged our presence. Pricilla seemed to be really enjoying this aspect. She loved it when people referred to her as Dr. Appleton. Jonathan was standing at the back door. A smile immediately came over my face.

"Dr. Petrot, do you have a moment?" asked Jonathan.

To my surprise, Jonathan was saving me. I had never been so happy to see someone. I must have been smiling from ear to ear.

"Yes, I have a minute! Dr. Appleton has a meeting that she must make. I also have a meeting, but we can talk quickly."

Pricilla grabbed my arm to force me to stop for a moment. She should really stop touching me. She came closer to me, so that only I could understand her, and said, "So, I guess someone was listening at your door."

"I doubt it."

"So, you texted him to meet you during this time, and I beat him by a few seconds," said Pricilla.

"You know that I went straight to class. When would I have had the time to text him? I have been teaching."

"Your shadow always shows up at the right moment," said Pricilla.

I pulled away forcibly from Pricilla and started walking quickly toward Jonathan.

"Bye, Pricilla. This round should go to me with the assist of Jonathan. I want to make sure that he gets credit."

"I thought he did not purposefully help you," said Pricilla.

"He did *not,* but students should always get credit."

"I concede this round, so I am coming back hardcore," declared Pricilla.

I could only imagine the rest of the day with her. I felt like I just entered the second round of a nightmare. I turned back to Jonathan with a calm demeanor.

"I have a meeting, but did you need something?"

"I know you do not like it when people gossip, but the rumor around campus is that you will be covering for Dr. Everstone's classes today and possibly tomorrow. Did you need me to do anything before the start of those classes?" asked Jonathan.

"When did you hear this?"

Talking fast, Jonathan stated, "This morning. It is all over the library. Remember, I started working there last month."

"I know. This is why I thought that you would be a good fit with Dr. Pimpleton."

"Mm. Well, it was all over school, but it was probably spread by Dr. Appleton's graduate assistant, Jennifer. She seems to know about everything," said Jonathan.

"It would be helpful to have an idea of what chapters they covered thus far, but this may be impossible to know before I reach the classes today. I may have to cover the classes until the end of the week."

Writing everything down quickly, Jonathan stated, "You have two hours before his block. I have an obligation within the block that should not take me long, so let me see what I can find out. Based on the information that I find out, I will mock up a semi-agenda and place it in your inbox. Two of the sections are introductory classes, and the last section is senior seminar."

"I forgot that this is his three-course term. I was only planning on covering the two introductory courses today. I guess I should have looked over the material before working with you this morning. I really was not worried about it. This also sounds like a lot of work. Do you think you can find out before I start?"

"Yes, especially since I am in senior seminar. One class down and you can do the introduction classes in your sleep. Marie covers those classes. I will reach out to her now," stated Jonathan.

"Did anyone tell Marie that she does not have to cover Dr. Everstone's classes today?"

"I think this is how the rumor got started. She is really close to Jennifer," stated Jonathan.

"Okay. I cannot be late for the meeting with the president. I will text you once I get out of that meeting."

"See you later. See, I am a good potato," said Jonathan, laughing.

"Is this our joke for today?"

"This is the last time that I am going to bring it up," articulated Jonathan.

"Good. Thank you for all your help."

"No problem. See you after your meeting," said Jonathan.

"I will text you once I am done."

I rushed down to the president's office. I had a feeling that she was not happy that she had to wait until I finished class. I walked into the presidential suite and greeted the administrative staff. The office always had at least two people but could have up to four administrative staff working for the upper echelon at the university.

In unison, everyone said, "Good morning."

"Good morning. How is everyone today?'

I received all types of responses, ranging from "good" to "My head kind of hurts, but it will be fine once I get my second cup of coffee." One of the voices asked how I was doing.

I was unable to recognize the voice, so I said to everyone, "I am fine, thank you." The ladies tried to engage me in light banter, but President Miller's administrative assistant informed me that the president was waiting for me and that I could go right into her office. She also informed me that Lieutenant Alenzo would be joining in about fifteen minutes. The urgency of the assistant's voice made me nervous. I felt like *I* was in trouble. I knocked on the door, waiting until she confirmed that I could enter.

"Good morning, President Miller."

"What's good about it, Rot?" asked President Miller.

"So, I assume that the board meeting did not go well."

"You figure," pronounced President Miller.

"Okay. I am just going to sit down in this huge, comfortable, leather chair and listen."

"We must talk quickly before Lieutenant Alenzo arrives. He is such a waste of space. His picture of arresting Ms. Walker has been all over the news," stated President Miller.

President Miller hated when the university was placed in a bad light under her watch.

"Did you talk to Ms. Walker? I know she made an appointment with your office."

"No," said President Miller.

"Did you decline the appointment?"

"I am really not sure," said President Miller.

"Okay. You must talk to her before she stages another protest."

"Why do you think that she will have another protest?" asked President Miller.

"Because she got the publicity that she desired from the first protest. It has been all over the local and national news. I told you she is quite aware that she cannot win the case, but she can embarrass Bron at the expense of the school. You must talk to her now. Can you get an appointment with her in the next hour?"

"This sounds like manipulation to me," declared President Miller.

"Is it manipulation, or will it be interpreted as a lack of leadership to the board?"

"Are you trying to tell me what to *do*?" asked President Miller.

"No. I would never fathom doing that, but you want to get ahead of this before the board makes some decisions for you. What was the reaction from the board?"

"No one was happy," proclaimed President Miller.

"I could have guessed that aspect. What else did they say?"

"Handle it. One member asked whether I found out what Maria wanted out of the situation. I did not have the answer. I lied and said that she had not specified anything yet, which was technically not a lie, but a reach of the truth," said President Miller.

"Have you talked to her this morning?"

"No. I thought you said that Bronston would take the job at the other university," stated President Miller.

"I said that he *may* take it and that you had to pitch it so he thought that it was his idea. Have you talked to him this morning?"

"No," proclaimed President Miller.

"He may be a little more amenable today."

"Did he say something to you?" asked President Miller.

"Me? No. But he did send me a death threat and confirmation that I was covering his classes."

"We, the board and I, did not want Marie doing anything extra.

This was a suggestion by the university attorney, but a point you made two weeks ago," said President Miller.

"I just thought that the optics may not be the most appropriate. Bron also informed Peaboy that I would be taking his position soon. How could he make that statement, especially since I have not received tenure yet?"

"I did not confirm that you had that position," asserted President Miller.

"I see."

"Look, I cannot worry about Bronston now, Rot. Ms. Walker is my focus. The media is still on my lawn and growing larger. You know that some of the outlets arrived before I got on campus?" asked President Miller.

"Yes. I did see them, and I arrived early."

"The board is not happy about this aspect. You did not tell me that Ms. Walker would stage a protest outside of the hearing building," articulated President Miller.

"I informed you that she was scheduled to do something on that hearing day."

"She did not file a form to stage a protest with the university," stated President Miller.

"Lack of preparation on her part or she could care less about the university policy."

"I have a feeling that you knew more," stated President Miller.

"I cannot be associated with any of these aspects. I have goals beyond the next few days."

"Yeah, I heard that line from Bronston," said President Miller.

"I have always been forthright concerning my aspirations. I am actually not that comfortable with having a meeting with you and Campus Security. But I am here. I do not want to be seen on any side of the issue."

"I will explain your presence to Lieutenant Alenzo upon his arrival," stated President Miller.

We heard a rustling at the door, and then, immediately, someone looked for a key. We both looked at each other for a split second. I guessed President Miller had locked her door. She did not want any surprises. The bigger surprise was that the intruder had no qualms about going quickly to find the key versus knocking. President Miller walked over to unlock the door.

"I came a little early, and I know from my son that Dr. Petrot always comes early. I assumed that you wanted to get a lot done," said Lieutenant Alenzo.

I guessed we were all going to ignore that he made no effort to knock on the door.

"Thank you. I included Dr. Petrot due to her experience with protest and her research on activist behavior. I believe that her insight will be helpful in this situation," said President Miller.

"I look forward to working with her," said Lieutenant Alenzo.

Lieutenant Alenzo really did not like me, but we both gave the impression to our boss, President Miller, that we were eager beavers looking forward to *this* journey. We talked for about forty minutes about a strategy to end the protest. But then we all heard music that was blasting. At first, we assumed it was something from the Campus Activities Board (CAB).

"I did not know that CAB had something planned today."

"Their event was not on my list," said Lieutenant Alenzo.

We heard the chime.

"You have a problem."

We rushed to the window. Everyone was in dark green on the lawn, except the media outlets stationed on the outside of the event.

You could see people for miles, especially since the president's office was up on a higher floor. The crowd included a rainbow of ages and identities. One little girl in her dark green shirt, holding her mother's hand, looked like she could be no older than five. People had various signs held up, ranging from *Protect Victims* to *Down with the Administration.* One individual had on a hood in the crowd. The person stood out because no one else had a hood. It seemed like the hooded helper from the first protest was also out. I tried to determine the culprit, but you could not determine the identity because the face was covered with some type of mesh. Everyone was looking in the direction of the president's office, but silent. All three of us were staring at them. They could see us.

"We need to do something now," forcibly stated President Miller.

"I am on it," said Lieutenant Alenzo.

"Wait. Take a breath."

"Why? We need to nip this in the bud now," stated Lieutenant Alenzo, rushing to the door.

"No. Wait. They want you to respond and arrest Ms. Walker. It is a flash mob. Everyone is in the same color. This had to be planned. It can only last for a few minutes."

The next few minutes seemed like forever, and they both looked at me intensely. Lieutenant Alenzo broke the silence and stated, "She is wrong, and she is wrong about a lot of things."

Both President Miller and I looked at the lieutenant because he was obviously making a reference to something else. I knew not to show a response. Leaders did not respond to negative comments. It showed weakness.

President Miller then turned to me and stated, "I think you underestimated this protest."

"Even with all her expertise," stated Lieutenant Alenzo as I shifted my gaze to him.

I took a moment and started counting to twenty in my head, but I did not respond directly to Lieutenant Alenzo. I, however, told them both, pointing to the window, "Look."

They both rushed to the window. Everyone was starting to move. Thank God. I also noticed that Lieutenant Alenzo tilted his head as if he noticed someone.

"It is a flash mob. It cannot last forever. It loses its emphasis if people stay there forever or for a long time."

"What?" questioned Lieutenant Alenzo, very upset that I was right.

Ms. Walker got on her bullhorn and stated, "I am coming out every day until the administration does something to make the campus safe, even if I am alone."

You could see people taking off their green shirts and putting on another clothing item or adjusting their outfit in some way. I recognized Pricilla. Her green shirt was distinctive. She always must stand out in a crowd, and she took a long time to change into her new outfit. She even had the nerve to take a few pictures before she started changing.

"Wonderful. The media is never going to get off the lawn," declared President Miller.

"The next few hours are important. I suggest contacting Ms. Walker and Marie to see what they want."

"No, we need a forceful response," said Lieutenant Alenzo.

"Has the force worked? It has resulted in media coverage. If Lieutenant Alenzo had rushed out, who would he have arrested? All the participants?"

"I would have arrested Ms. Walker," said Lieutenant Alenzo.

"And you would have fed into her narrative. The narrative needs to change."

The president was not happy, but she was listening to me. Like myself, she had to have seen the interview last night and this morning with Ms. Walker. She had been on three different outlets since the protest yesterday.

"Look, this was planned, and everyone made sure that they looked different quickly. The school would have looked horrible. I could only imagine those images."

"I realize that now," whispered Lieutenant Alenzo.

President Miller stared at me for a moment like I knew that this protest was going to happen, and she was mad at me. In fact, her eyes were filled with rage, but her words did not indicate her anger when she said, "Thank you, Dr. Petrot. We would have made a huge mistake."

The silence for those few seconds was thick. They both seemed frustrated with me. I did not start the protest, and in fact, I had helped them. President Miller's administrative assistant burst into the office, another person that did not knock, and told President Miller that the phone was ringing off the hook, and several calls were from board members.

"I have to do some damage control," stated President Miller.

"I am going to go."

"Did you want us to return later?" asked Lieutenant Alenzo, trying to gain favor with President Miller.

"I have to put out some fires out now, so stay, Lieutenant Alenzo, to help me," stated President Miller.

I started to put some fire in my step. I had crossed a line, but President Miller had drawn it.

"Dr. Petrot, I will be trying to find you later today," said President Miller.

"As you know, I am covering for Dr. Everstone's classes besides my own, so I may be teaching class."

"I will have my admin track down your schedule and find an open spot. It may be late tonight after you are done. I assume that I will not be leaving the campus any time soon," said President Miller.

"I will be around."

As I walked out of the office, I could hear President Miller saying to Lieutenant Alenzo, I assumed, because she was not whispering, "You notice that she did not respond to your petty comments. You looked interesting at those moments. Do you have an issue with Dr. Petrot? Do not answer my question. Just get over it because she will be in leadership soon."

The door closed, and I could not hear his response. I walked out of the suite and toward the cafeteria. I did not grab the lunch that my aunt made for me, so I had to grab something to eat in the unhealthy cesspool we called the cafeteria. I peeked around a couple of corners trying to make sure that I did not bump into Pricilla. I did notice Jo walking towards me. She purposely made an emphasis to fake-bump into me.

"Stop playing."

"I figured that you would appreciate the joke since you love it when people touch you," said Jo.

"Everyone has jokes today."

"Before we start talking about something else, how is your aunt doing? I know she had a cold."

"It was not COVID. She is fine. She divides her time between me and her *new* man now."

"What? Aunt Marlene got a man?" said Jo inquisitively.

"Yeah, this old guy. He is kind of cute for a crypt keeper. She kept him hidden for a minute. Do not underestimate how Petrot women can keep a secret. He has a little bit of money too. He wants to marry her."

"Really?" asked Jo, laughing.

"You know that is the only reason why she told me. She would have kept him secret until the end of time by acting like she was going to church events. Bingo or some prayer group event does not occur *every* night. How much prayer can you do?"

"You know that comment was wrong," said Jo.

"Okay, but I have been letting her keep up her little illusion up for a while. The excuses were so interesting *to me*. She was quite creative on some evenings. I knew she would have to tell me at some point."

"He has no idea what he is asking for. He cannot afford her," said Jo, cracking up.

"*I know*. Her monthly purse allowance alone is crazy. How many purses can one really carry in one month?"

"I guess the same number of shoes that you can use in one month," laughed Jo.

"Boy, the jokes are really flowing today."

"You know that people would kill for two months of your shoe collection, especially Pricilla," stated Jo, bending over laughing.

"You are so funny today."

Jo leaned forward, acting serious, and whispered, "I heard that you and Pricilla are playing a game, and she lost the first round. Did you see her in her green shirt?"

"You are so funny today. She is playing with fire. You know she was taking pictures of herself at the protest to the side. This was the only reason that she participated in the protest. I would bet money that she is posting it on Facebook to show her involvement."

"I guess she is not worried about the note we got from administration," said Jo.

"She probably did not read it fully."

Laughing at a lower volume, Jo said, "I have no doubt of that. I think deep down she likes the attention. I do not think that she could withstand the attention of her true issue coming out, however. She is determined to do anything to be in this group and secure her spot."

"I have heard this point."

"I think you are underestimating her determination to remove Marcus by any means necessary. Which we may need since he has decided to become a problem. So, the meeting tonight starts at 6:00 p.m. I moved it up. We will both be done with our block, and we will have fifteen minutes to get to the meeting. I am assuming that you have not seen my email yet. Pricilla told me that you had a meeting with the president today," stated Jo.

"She can never stop gossiping. Is it possible?"

"No, this is a fact of her personality," said Jo.

"Wow."

"I know you are covering Bron's classes, by way of Pricilla also," stated Jo.

"Sure you do."

"So just stay after your last class. I wanted to accommodate your long day," said Jo.

"I would prefer to move the grant meeting until tomorrow. We need to deal with *our* situation today."

"I am going to ignore your response. We can walk and chew gum. Ponder this. We must get the group moving to meet the deadline, and I know you hate to rush," declared Jo.

"True, but I was supposed to bring Marcus as my surprise guest. I will tell him the meeting will start at seven."

"I am not worried. One of the group members will make him feel so uncomfortable at the meeting that he will not make it to the end of the meeting," stated Jo, turning and booking it to her class. She turned quickly back to me to catch my glare and said, "See you tonight."

I grabbed my lunch, unfortunately unhealthy, and started walking to my office. I peeked around a couple of corners, trying to make sure that I did not bump into Pricilla. I guess she needed to get rid of her evidence. To my surprise, both Ms. Walker and Marie were at my back door.

"Ladies, due to recent activities, I cannot talk to either of you without my faculty representative."

The university legal team, late last night, after the first protest, sent a stern cautionary note outlining the university's position and consequences of employee or student involvement in the current situation.

"Is that like a union representative?" asked Marie.

"Yes."

"You do not have to talk. I will do all the talking, Ms. Attorney," said Ms. Walker.

I wanted to correct her. If she was going to insult me, at least call me Dr. Attorney.

"Mom, I got this," stated Marie.

I turned to Marie and said nothing. Silence was often underrated by most.

"Everyone in the crowd saw you in the president's office this morning. I thought you were helping us. You provided us with so many options over the last month," said Marie.

"This statement is incorrect. I did not personally provide you or your legal counsel with anything. I am not part of your legal team."

Clearing her throat and making sure that she had the correct wording, Marie pronounced, "I meant to say that we gained information that we assumed was from you."

"Please do not assume that I sent you anything. I cannot be involved in this situation. This is a matter with the university and involves specific policy and procedure."

Shifting her weight from one side to the other, Ms. Walker shouted, "This is not stern enough. People are starting to question whether Marie is telling the truth since they saw you in the window today."

"There is no need to yell at me. Ladies, due to recent activities, I cannot talk to either of you without my faculty representative."

Lowering her voice only a bit and leaning forward, Ms. Walker said, "Marie is standing in this situation because of YOU."

"This statement is untrue. I have never provided you with anything directly. I have not been a part of any of the process thus far. A sexual misconduct incident is handled by the Title IX coordinator. I am not that person."

"We know that you are not that person," barked Ms. Walker.

"So, I guess I am a little lost on how this is my fault. I feel as if you are placing me in an uncomfortable situation based on my activism and research."

"Oh, so now you are going to play the victim card," roared Ms. Walker.

"Marie and I have worked together in the past, but I have no desire to be entangled with the current situation."

I felt confident that many ears were listening to our conversation. We all stood there for a moment in silence. I got the feeling that the silence was bothering them both. I guessed they assumed that I would say something. I did not, and I started walking closer to my door. However, the two ladies were blocking it.

"Look, you backstabber. The first two events should have changed the tide for my daughter. The university should have contacted one of us by now," blared Ms. Walker in a lower tone to match mine.

"I have studied your activism and research work. The two protests should have created two situations," stated Marie.

I tilted my head a bit to hear these revelations but said nothing.

Marie leaned forward so the three of us only heard her and said, "The fraternity should have come out on the lawn to fight back. They would have been arrested with my mom. And Campus Security should have come to arrest us today. Both populations would have increased the media presence on campus and my leverage."

"Ladies, due to recent activities, I cannot talk to either of you without my faculty representative."

"Shut up. You are driving me crazy with that line," declared Ms. Walker.

I stepped back away from my door. Ms. Walker's behavior seemed to be taking a turn, and I was a little worried about my physical safety. She towered over me a bit and was about thirty pounds heavier. I had to be in a proper stance to defend myself.

"Ms. Walker, I can sense that you are upset, but I have nothing to do with administration. In fact, I am just a non-tenured faculty member."

"Who holds a lot of power on campus. Your presentations have been packed, especially this week. I heard that you have a new book coming out in a few months. I would assume that this situation has boosted your other lines of income—book, podcast. People look up to you and follow your lead," said Marie.

"The new book was slated for next month. It just happens that the book deals with the same topic. Remember, I am up for tenure, and this publication boosts my review. I am just *one* faculty member in *one* department."

"STOP acting like you have no influence on campus," screeched Ms. Walker.

"I do not have any influence. I am not part of administration."

155

"YET. So, why were you in the president's office?" asked Ms. Walker. My phone started ringing, which did break the tension for a bit.

"For a meeting."

"A perfect statement by an attorney. You are always covering yourself," stated Ms. Walker angrily.

"I thought you supported me," uttered Marie, looking distressed.

"Ladies, sexual misconduct cases go through specific channels. I am not part of that process."

Ms. Walker got closer to me again and stated, "She based her entire movements on your lectures, activism, and research work."

"I thought you supported me," uttered Marie.

The hallway was totally silent due to students being in class, but I also knew that ears were listening to the conversation. It was so silent that someone could have dropped a pin in their office, and we would have heard it.

"Ladies, due to recent activities, as stated before, I cannot engage in this conversation with you both without my faculty representative, and I must leave at this juncture. I cannot confirm or deny support for either side without placing my job at risk."

I eased past both women without making contact, which was quite difficult. I began to unlock my back door. I could hear someone banging on my front door. I assumed it was Pricilla. My phone started ringing again. Pricilla could not be on the phone. She did not have the number. Someone was really trying to get in touch with me.

Ms. Walker's behavior shifted into overdrive, and she shouted, "Marie is standing in this position because of you. I blame you. The devil will get his money. But I am coming for you, NOW."

Ms. Walker began to lunge at me, but I quickly shifted and barely slid into my office as Marie grabbed her mother. I could see her fist as I closed it. I needed to file the incident with Campus Security immediately. I now had to add this to my list of tasks for the day. I was so interested in talking to Lieutenant Alenzo about this situation. *I imagined having so much fun.*

"Your day is coming," said Ms. Walker through the closed door.

I wondered how long they both would stand at a closed door. Ms. Walker started a steady but consistent knock on the door for a few minutes. I had no choice but to ignore it as I took a moment to catch my breath. Her punch almost landed. My colleagues could be so helpful. No one thought to call Security to remove this woman. I could hear Marie calming her mother down.

Through the door, Ms. Walker shouted, "I am going to find you *TODAY.* No, tonight. I know what your car looks like, and you are parked in the back lot. This whole thing will be settled tonight. And everyone knows that you are covering Dr. Everstone's classes and not Marie, so I know you will be in the building late."

Okay. I definitely had to get the escort to my car tonight. I did not get the feeling that Ms. Walker made unsupported threats. The knocking on my front door began again. Could this possibly be Security? I opened the front door with minimal hope that it was Security, and my phone began to ring again. I was not late for anything, so I had no idea who was ringing. I gave my private number to very few people, and I really did not think that it was my aunt. She did not use the emergency code system, so I knew that it was not her, and Jo was in class.

My good *friend* Bron was standing at the front door. *Could the day get any better?*

"*Making friends,*" said Bron.

"More than you, Mama's Boy. What are you doing here?"

Bron got closer to me, which caused me to move back a bit, and said, "Have you opened your email yet?"

This was weird. Bron was talking to me in a halfway normal manner. The Marcus situation must have escalated.

"You know the answer to that question is no. I just got finished teaching. And since you are here, you can teach your own classes."

"No, Dr. Peaboy assigned them to you," replied Bron.

"What the heck?"

Bron got closer to me, looked me directly in my eyes, and whispered, "Check your email, *now*."

He walked away without making a smart remark. I knew that something was wrong. I hurriedly went to my desk. This email must have been something, but I also wanted to know who was blowing up my phone. I opened my bag and looked down at my phone first. The message and several texts were from Mrs. Everstone. I then assumed that the email message was from Bron's mother. He was just delivering the demand to answer my phone now, and she did not appreciate that I did not answer *her* on my private line. I went to my computer. To my shock, the message was not from Mrs. Everstone or Pricilla, but from Marcus. The message to the three of us said, "I know what you did in the past, and I can prove it."

Chapter Thirteen
Dr. Bronston Everstone

LATER IN THE DAY...

ould the day get any worse? I had to talk to my current nemesis. I needed to confirm that Rot got the same message from Marcus that I did. I knew that all our names were in the message, but I needed confirmation. Of course, she knew my personality, so she sent a message. I got it, and we would deal with it tonight.

I had not heard from Jo yet. I emailed her earlier about the message. I decided to walk to Jo's office, but of course in the hallway outside of the office suite, after passing a few people, I bumped into the gossip queen, even though the hallway was quite spacious.

In a conversational tone, Pricilla said, "Hello, Bronston. I did not think that I would see you today. Is Petrot in her office?"

"Not now, Pricilla. Go check for yourself."

"No need to be rude," uttered Pricilla.

"Whatever."

Forcing me to pause for a moment by grabbing my forearm, Pricilla asked, "Since you are here today, does that mean that you will be teaching your classes today?"

Pricilla tended to place her hands on people without even thinking about it. This seemed unusual to me, especially since she worked in the counseling center. What happened to consent? Men were automatically criticized for consent, but how about women? I could feel violated.

"Do you ever get off the gossip train? You cannot help yourself. It is a flaw in your character. It is none of your business. You do not have to cover me today, so why do *YOU* care?"

"I am just trying to determine Petrot's schedule. I need to talk to her before the meeting. You will be at the meeting, right?" asked Pricilla.

"You know I will be at the meeting. I feel confident that Jo already made that confirmation with you. Probably early this morning."

Ignoring my previous comment, Pricilla asked, "You know that the meeting time changed to 6:00 p.m. Right?"

"Yes, to accommodate both Jo's and Rot's schedule. I did fully read the email from Jo."

Pricilla was so hard to stomach. Jo was the buffer. Pricilla usually had about two minutes before I told her about herself.

In a jovial voice, trying to be upbeat, Pricilla said, "I just wanted to confirm your attendance and your confirmation of not including Marcus."

I knew that if Marcus was included, either Alfred or Pricilla would be cut. I opted at that moment to be a pain.

"I see no problem with Marcus. He is harmless and quiet. He will do what he is told to do with little if any pushback. Rot may have a great suggestion. He seems to be the perfect person for the team."

"If I am not mistaken, she opted to get rid of you also," expressed Pricilla, visually making eye contact with my tie.

"I am not worried. I come with benefits."

"Not after the protest today," said Pricilla with a bold tone.

"Are you going there with *me* today? I would not want to have a repeat of the holiday party. And no, I did not touch you. You touched me first. I just had a response to a lubricated person touching me. I do not have to *physically touch* you for *you* to have problems."

Trying to limit my movement, especially since the hallway was empty now, Pricilla said in a lower tone, "No. This conversation is going in the wrong direction. I just want to point out that I have had many publications recently. I am one of the leading scholars presently in my field, unlike Marcus. I offer many different aspects to the team, and I will do *anything* to be on the team."

"I have to go."

"Have a great day," emitted Pricilla.

It was like Pricilla did not hear half the conversation. She walked down to Rot's back door. I heard Rot open the door slightly at first and say, "Heck, no," and shut the door immediately. I knew that Pricilla had enough sense not to knock again on the door. I kept walking for fear that Pricilla would catch up and try to keep talking. I had to make it to Jo's office without her. I needed to talk to Jo alone.

I could not believe that Marcus was trying to force his way onto this research grant. He was on the student service side; he did not need the grant to supplement his portfolio for a tenure package or anything else. I was not a fan of Marcus. He creeped me out. I did not like the way that he looked at me and especially the way that he looked at Jo. He was a creep.

I knocked on Jo's door, but she did not answer. I knocked again, indicating that it was me. Brown popped up. I assumed that he walked up, but he was always around Jo or not very far. Her husband once mentioned this aspect to both Rot and me at dinner at their home one evening. Jo told us all to ignore this aspect, which I had heard a couple of times in graduate school. Brown was not the first man and would not be the last to be completely consumed and obsessed with Jo. This was code from Jo to drop the conversation, which included not just the two of us, but also her husband. Since Brown was currently at her door, I assumed that Jo would be coming soon. He knew her schedule backwards and forwards. I would not be startled to find out that Brown had a shrine in both his office and home dedicated to Jo.

"Jo is in class. She sent us a message that both she and Rot would be teaching until our meeting tonight. You may not have gotten it," said Brown.

"That's right. They both will not be available until that meeting."

Unlike Pricilla, Brown did not mention my presence on campus today. He knew to stay in his lane. This was an aspect that Jo mentioned to both Rot and me.

"Did you need me to do something in preparation for the meeting?" asked Brown.

"No. I am set for the meeting."

"Do you have a moment to talk?" asked Brown.

Maybe Jo was mistaken about Brown. This request was a little unsettling. My current situation placed me in an awkward situation around campus, but I was not looking for new friends.

"About what?"

"Marcus," said Brown.

This piqued my interest. I knew he did not get the same email that the three of us had gotten, but I needed to make sure. I decided to play along and talk to him for a moment.

"Sure. Did you want to meet me in my office in a few minutes? I only have a few minutes, though."

Brown gleamed with excitement and said, "YES." He tried to play off his response after I gave him a strange look. He looked like the kid at the playground that was chosen last, but who had gotten chosen first in that one special incident.

"Give me about ten minutes to get back to my office. I need to do a few things."

"Okay. I will be there," declared Brown with emphasis.

He would be there. I thought it was important to always make people wait. I also did not want to walk around campus with him. I already had an image issue. I did not need to add a Brown issue to this situation. He had interesting social skills. But I had to give him credit—he was well-known in Homeland Security. Jo was correct in suggesting him for a spot on the team. I had to figure out how to get a message to Jo in between her classes. It would look weird for me to be hanging out at her classroom door. My phone ringing distracted me as I opened my office door.

"Hello."

"I need to talk to you," responded President Miller.

"I need to talk to Brown quickly. It will not take long. I can be in your office in fifteen minutes."

"I am assuming that it is a part of your research project because he is on the team. But are you on campus or on Zoom with Brown? Because I know that Brown is not at your house," asked President Miller.

"Yes."

"Which one?" questioned President Miller. I could sense over the line that she was getting perturbed. I had experienced this response over another situation from our past in working with a past donor, and I did not want to replay that record in this lifetime again.

"I am on campus."

"I thought Dr. Petrot was covering your classes because you have obligations today and tomorrow. Is she in her office now?" asked President Miller.

"I do, but I am handling a few things on campus now."

"Just walk down once you are finished with Brown," said President Miller, shifting her tone a bit.

"You are not going to give me the option of bringing my attorney?"

"Walk down if you want, but I would suggest that you walk down alone. Up to you, however. We *all* still have options, but that door is closing," said President Miller before she hung up on me.

Another woman hanging up on me. My mother started this trend. I looked out of the window and pondered whether I should call my attorney, my mother, or even Malcolm. I had a feeling that President Miller would show me my options, but not with anyone with me. All I had to do at this juncture was listen. I also had a bigger problem—Marcus. He was making reference to my past. I could not let my past interfere with my future, regardless of whether it looked bright at the moment. Brown slightly knocked before walking through the door.

"Do you have a habit of walking into a room without permission?"

The smile from Brown's face disappeared quickly. He paused for a moment and looked around. I got the feeling that he was trying to look for a location to hide. I needed to assess this current situation with Marcus, so I changed my tone.

"I am only joking. We *may* be working together soon. Come in, Brown."

"Oh, the joke was funny," said Brown, trying to match my tone.

I immediately got the feeling that Brown did not have many friends, and I knew that he did not pledge. The brothers would have broken him of the habit of taking any situation given to you.

"Have a seat."

Brown looked at me with caution. I assumed he thought that another shoe would be dropping soon. "I just wanted to take a moment to talk about Marcus," said Brown.

"What about him?"

"I know that he is trying to get on this team, but I see no reason to add him," stated Brown.

"If I am not mistaken, *your* position is not secure at this moment." I figured that there was no need for me to be totally nice to him.

"I am not sure if you are aware, but I secured another support letter for the project," said Brown.

"I was unaware of this aspect, but do you think this will be enough for Rot?"

"I do not want to take thunder away from Jo if she was going to announce this letter later," said Brown.

He was opting to ignore the Rot comment and play games. This was a running theme today from everyone.

"I do not think that Jo is worried about *you* telling me about the letter." I figured that I would play along with Brown's game. The focus was to find out if he had gotten an email from Marcus today.

"I have concerns about Marcus's work output. The university denied him a promotion. This would indicate that he is not reaching a level of excellence," articulated Brown.

"Good point, so you think that Pricilla would be the most appropriate team member?"

Straightening his back in his chair, Brown said, "Yes."

"You do not have concerns about her level of dissemination of information?"

"It can be seen as a downfall but would be overshadowed by her work output. I am not sure if you are aware, but she has a publication coming out this month. It is in one of the top journals in her field," proclaimed Brown.

"Yeah. I heard about this aspect. I also know that Jo and Rot helped her with that publication. They knew that she would need it for the promotion, so they did not add their names."

"I did not know about this aspect. Petrot could have used it for her current tenure review this year and Jo in the next two," declared Brown.

"It was important to make the investment into Pricilla at that juncture. She needed the publication more for her package and to be the sole author. This is why we surround our unit with the best."

"I know," uttered Brown.

"So, let's continue with our conversation. I have to go to another meeting soon."

"I am so sorry to be holding you up," stated Brown as he kept nervously palming his hands.

"I wanted to take the moment to talk to you. Did you have anything else to tell me about Marcus? Have you heard anything from Marcus today?"

"No," said Brown, pausing and sighing after his response.

"Why the sigh and pause?"

"Well, I have not heard from him today, but…" said Brown, still palming his hands.

"But what? Was he sending emails to encourage you to convince us to have him join the team?"

"No. But I think it is also important to consider personalities when forming a team. I have concerned that Marcus's personality will not mesh with everyone on the team," asserted Brown.

"What are you talking about?"

"I just think that Marcus does not generate a solid work product from others, and it may be due to his personality," championed Brown.

"Are you friends?"

"No," uttered Brown.

I looked at him for a moment. Brown moved uneasily in his seat. I figured that I should stay quiet because his next statement should be interesting.

"I may not have many colleagues as friends on campus, but Marcus is also not friends with Jo. She is friends with everyone, and she works with Pricilla. There is no need to add a variable that may hurt the unit and production. I would take care to remove any aspect that hurts the unit, but there is not a need to add a negative when a positive is available," proclaimed Brown.

I got the feeling that Brown was not talking about us all, but just Jo. I also knew that he would protect Jo at all costs. Brown served his purpose for me at this moment. He could go. I just needed the best way to kick him out somewhat nicely. I knew that he would be on the team after tonight. I had no intention of running all the statistics for all the projects that would be decided by Rot, and I did not want to inform him of my meeting with the president. There was no need to inject him into *that* conversation.

"I have to go to my next meeting."

"Thank you for talking to me. I look forward to seeing you tonight," said Brown.

"See you tonight."

Brown walked out my office, and I gathered myself for the meeting with the president. I took the moment to acknowledge each person in President Miller's office, while I was turning off my phone. My mother always taught me to take a moment to say hello. It was just good manners and often served me well. President Miller's administrative assistant looked quite flustered but informed me that I could go right into the office. I knew that once I closed the door, the office would be buzzing with conversation about me. But a portion of the conversation would include that my appearance and stature, regardless of the situation, was flawless. Another aspect that my mother taught me—to never let them see you sweat.

"Hello."

"Sit down, Bronston," said President Miller.

"Okay. How may I help you on this fine afternoon?"

"Please do not take that tone with me," stated President Miller.

"You called the meeting."

"What are you going to do about today?" asked President Miller.

"What are you going to do about today? You and Rot did not come up with a plan yet?"

"You know that she is covering your classes and will not be done until late tonight after your meeting," stated President Miller.

"How do you know about the meeting?"

"Jo, of course. I wrote one of your letters. I heard that Brown secured another letter for you application," verbalized President Miller.

"So, you expect that I will beat this situation now?"

"I now know how powerful your mother is in this community and exactly how many friends she has on and off our board," uttered President Miller.

"You have always known my family's reach. Why now?"

"The media circus hurt Ms. Walker. We cannot have the media on the lawn searching for the answer when this all can be decided behind closed doors. The media is being blamed on Ms. Walker and not on you and your legal team," said President Miller.

"Go figure. A narrative is powerful. What is the board suggesting?"

"To solve this situation without an official decision and to get Ms. Walker off the lawn. Are you sure that you do not want to take the other job?" asked President Miller.

"Good try, but no. This is my home, and I have done nothing."

"Okay, I need to go to Plan D," articulated President Miller.

"That is a phrase that Rot would use. I would watch my back around her. Do you even have a Plan D? Or are you waiting until after our team meeting to get a Plan D? Or are you waiting to receive an email or text from Rot with a suggestion?"

"No, but I do know that Plan D includes Ms. Walker," stated President Miller.

"I did not do this."

"That may be the truth, but we are in different waters now. I will find you all after your team meeting tonight."

"Wow, you have changed after working with Rot. Always looking now for the best angel to place yourself in the best light?"

"I should not protect myself. And speaking of that—Dr. Pimpleton made an effort to find me today in all this chaos. He informed me that he would be joining your team, and his membership was supported by all three of you. He mentioned how a past picture brought to light your friendship from graduate school. Do you know what he is talking about?" asked President Miller.

"We are pondering his membership on the team."

I did not want to tip my hand concerning Marcus, and I knew that Rot would never let President Miller into our inner circle. Even though she was allowed to use her nickname, and President Miller was making every effort in this conversation not to slip and use it, she was not part of the collective.

"Hence me looking for Dr. Petrot when I thought she was not going to cover your classes to gain clarification concerning the membership," declared President Miller.

"Was that the only reason you were looking for her and not Jo?" I knew that she would lie and say yes.

"Yes. Anyway, I am not a fan of Dr. Pimpleton. In fact, I was pushing for his termination. At other universities, student affairs staff are publishing articles in their field," said President Miller.

"True."

"I do not see his benefit. I was surprised when Dr. Petrot convinced him to stay," articulated President Miller.

"Rot has a plan for everything. It would be wise for you to remember this aspect, so are we done?"

"For now, but I will see you tonight," said President Miller.

"I assume that after the meeting tonight, my mother will be giving me some good news."

"Must be nice to have money," said President Miller.

"I have the truth."

I walked toward the door, fuming. I was sick and tired of people *not* believing me, but I got my composure before I opened the door. I did not want the presidential suite to have new "tea" to add to the gossip line.

"Have a great day, everyone."

In unison, everyone looked up, acting as if they had not recently kept quiet to hear the conversation between President Miller and me, and said some form of bye. I closed the door. I had a couple of hours, but I needed to track down Jo. I turned my phone back on. I did not want anyone to disturb our conversation. As my phone turned on, it blew up. I assumed that it was my mother. She would be furious that I turned off my phone. Besides my mother, the most was from Malcolm. He was furious. He informed me that Marcus had arrived at our exclusive country club looking for me, not looking the part at all.

Malcolm described him as a disheveled homeless man looking for a handout of food and clothing. Marcus could not find me, so he joined Malcolm for lunch instead and mentioned me as though we were great friends over thirty times. Malcolm was furious but would not show his disgust to any of the members. He also texted his assistant to purchase a jacket and another trinket in the store at the start of lunch. His assistant got it to Malcolm quickly. He was afraid of Malcolm but had lasted for almost a year. Malcolm gave them both to Marcus, stating that it was customary to buy a gift for a visiting friend, especially on their first visit to the club. Marcus brought the lie and immediately put on the jacket, which was the true objective.

Marcus had lost his mind. I needed to deal with my mother, Malcolm, and especially Marcus. The phone rang. It was my mother.

"Do not turn off your phone again," said my mother and hung up.

She had been hanging up on me for the last few days. She made a statement and hung up. How many women were going to hang up on me *today*? I knew that she would call me back later, but she could have said hello. I could have been in a very important meeting. My phone vibrated. It was a message from my lawyer. "Please contact your mother. She has been unable to contact you." No joke, Sherlock. The phone rang this time. It was Malcolm.

"What the hell?" asked Malcolm.

"I cannot talk about it over the phone."

"Is this a problem? You know that I had to go to the driving range with this guy. We were there for over an hour," said Malcolm.

"Over an hour?"

"Yes, and since when have the two of you been best friends?" shouted Malcolm.

"He said best friends."

"Yes. This is the reason that I went to the range with him. I needed to meet your best friend. And no need for other people to hear comments like that," declared Malcolm.

"You are sure he said best friends. He included Rot and Jo in the story. He said that the past came to light, and you all could not forget about your bond in graduate school. What bond?" stated Malcolm.

"I am going to take care of it tonight."

"Take care of what?" asked Malcolm.

"Not over the phone."

"Find me tonight," urged Malcolm.

"I have a team meeting, but I will find you."

"No, I will come to campus now. You will tell me what's going on now, and we will take care of it now," said Malcolm.

Malcolm could be very determined.

"No, I have to deal with some aspects which will take me up to the team meeting. I will be done around 8:00 p.m."

"I will be there before eight. I will wait for you. Just text once you're done. I do not like this situation," declared Malcolm.

"I caught it." Malcolm could be so driven, and he hated when someone said that he was not my best friend. Marcus got under his skin, especially after he could not resolve the Marie situation on the lawn.

Wait, Jo had a fifteen-minute break to get from her one class to her last class before the meeting. She always talked to students after class, which made her a little bit late. I rushed to her first class location. The students started coming out of the room. I waited for a few minutes.

After a few more minutes, I walked into the classroom. Jo was not in the room. I asked one of the students, "Where is Dr. Taylor?"

"She got an emergency text one hour into the class, walked out of the room, and talked to Dr. Petrot for a few seconds. She and Dr. Petrot came back into the room and stated that they were trying a new exercise that included both classes, which I assume would be your class actually, really. They framed it as a combination between criminology and sociology. Dr. Taylor passed out directions for an exercise for us to complete before the start of the next class. She allowed us to start at that moment, so we could have stayed in the room or completed it elsewhere," said the student.

"Did she leave with Dr. Petrot?"

"Yes," said the student.

"Thank you for the information." You thought that students were not listening or looking outside of a classroom. They looked at everything.

I got another text, which was in our group text message box. "We need to *take care* of our new friend, who has been seeing the light. We are assigning the classes an exercise that will allow us both to be at the meeting a little earlier. We pulled the exercise from our graduate school days. Marcus still thinks that the meeting will start at seven."

Chapter Fourteen
Dr. Joanna Taylor

LATE THAT NIGHT

I looked around the lobby of the library. I was specifically looking for Rot. She should have been here by now. I did, however, notice Marie at the desk. I had specifically chosen a day on which she would not be working. I did not want Bron to have to deal with her, and this was the real reason why I did not want to have the meeting tomorrow. Why was she here? I looked around to make sure that her mother was not around. I had a horrible sick feeling that they might have been staging another protest. This was the last thing that we needed tonight. And where was Rot? She was so concise with her presentations. She would be able to shave off another ten minutes of her lecture and still make sure that the students had the content.

Her group exercise was priceless. This was exactly why she had one of the highest SRTEs within her department and across campus. She determined a goal, and now she made it so all three of us could talk before the meeting. We needed to make sure that Marcus left the meeting before it ended. He needed to disqualify himself before we took care of him later. The text from Bron was incoherent, but my takeaway was that Marcus was using our names to raise his status on campus and in the community.

Rot hated when people stood on her back without permission. I knew she was having flashbacks to our graduate school days and working for her chair. She ensured that we walked away with something after slaving for that man, but she promised us both that we would never be in that situation again. The night she made that statement made me nervous, but the man was still alive and well. He, however, had not published anything since. He always asked about Rot at conferences that included both sociology and criminal justice peers, but I thought he was just trying to confirm her location. She never spoke ill of the man in public on the national academic stage, but her silence indicated something to everyone that knew her. Once she graduated, she made that man's life a living hell. The school did not strip him of his title, but he did lose his status, which was huge in an academic environment. Your name meant everything. She informed me that she wanted to make sure that I was fine for my last year and that I did not receive any backlash. I was not worried about it. She was handling it. This was why I did not understand why Bron would not follow Rot in some instances. He did not have to follow constantly but stay in his lane.

I was thankful that I had prepared the agenda for the team meeting last night and that I had contacted Jonathan four days before. He was the person who checked and made sure that Marie was not working. Either he made a mistake, or Marie switched with someone, but, again, why? If she and her mother started another protest in this library, I was going to go off. I really did not need this tonight.

"Good evening, Dr. Taylor," said Jonathan.

He startled me. I was totally focused on something else.

"Good evening, Jonathan. What is Marie doing here? Dr. Everstone will be here shortly. I do not want to have any problems."

"She switched with Jennifer," replied Jonathan.

"Why? Please do not tell me that another protest is going to occur tonight."

"Not that I am aware of," said Jonathan.

"This is not a good situation."

"Do not worry. I am the shift supervisor. I will move her to the fourth floor. Your meeting is on the third floor. She will never see Dr. Everstone. I will do it now," stated Jonathan.

"Oh, good."

"I want to make sure that I am providing you with everything that you need. Dr. Petrot would be upset if I did not give you the same level of service as I provide her," articulated Jonathan.

"Thank you."

"I will have my phone with me, so I will wait until I get your message about the grant group. I will stay on the first floor to ensure that you do not have any problems," said Jonathan.

"I just want Dr. Petrot to give the official okay for you to attend the meeting and to be one of our student workers. You may not get the text tonight because we must settle some other matters."

He had no idea of how many balls I had in the air at the moment. I wanted to make Rot happy, so I knew that including her shadow on the project would fit the bill. I also knew that Jonathan needed the money. College students never had money.

Looking down at the floor and looking sad, Jonathan said, "Okay."

The poor boy was in love with Rot. She might need to cut him loose. I had seen that look in other suitors, and it never turned out good. This was the reason why I ignored Alfred. He did not give me that look.

"Can you also do me another favor?"

"Sure, anything," said Jonathan.

"Can you text me once Dr. Pimpleton arrives in the building?"

"He is already in the building, and he had requested that I text him once Dr. Petrot arrived. He informed me that they have been good friends since graduate school," said Jonathan.

"Oh, really. Did you do that?"

"No, good friends text each other. Dr. Petrot informed me that she would be talking to him at seven," said Jonathan.

"Okay."

"He will receive a text closer to seven. I told him that I would send a text," said Jonathan.

"So, let me get this straight. Is Dr. Petrot in the building?"

"Yes, but I did not send a text to Dr. Pimpleton. I work for Dr. Petrot," said Jonathan in a calm voice, tilting his head to the side.

"Okay. I am going up to the third floor. Does she know the location of the meeting?"

"Yes," replied Jonathan.

I looked at him for a minute. His demeanor did not change. He was just telling me about the information in a factual manner like presenting a case in court.

"I must go then. She is probably already in the room waiting for me."

"The room has been open for a while," said Jonathan in a lower voice. "I will remove Marie."

"Thank you." I rushed to the room as soon as the elevator doors opened, but Rot was not in the room, and neither was her Vera bag and coat. My heart sank; I felt a chill come over me. Alfred startled me.

"You frightened me. What are you doing here?"

"Why? We have a meeting," said Alfred.

"I was not expecting you this early."

"I have been in the library working on some items, and I secured two more letters for you," said Alfred.

"That is wonderful. Rot will be happy about the letters. Do you have them on you?"

Alfred's happy face turned into a sad face.

"You know that Rot likes proof."

"I will go down to the computer lab and print out a copy. It will only take me a few minutes," said Alfred.

"Alfred, Rot will be really happy about the letters."

Alfred was ecstatic. He reached out to hug me but stopped in his tracks.

"I learned that I must request a hug. May I hug you?" asked Alfred.

"Let's start with a fist-bump. I appreciate that you made the request. You read Rot's pamphlet about consent."

We fist-bumped, and Alfred said, "Yes. I must hurry. I do not want to be late for the meeting."

"Why are you here so early?" asked Bron as he burst into the room, disheveled and out of breath.

"I figured that I could help Jo set up for the meeting, but I must go get something. I will be back," replied Alfred.

Bron and I both looked at each other as Alfred whisked out of the room. The three of us needed to talk before Marcus came into the room. Rot and I really did not get a chance to talk earlier. We had been surrounded by ears, who loved to listen and read lips. Rot only updated me quickly concerning the class exercise. I just followed her lead.

"We only have a few minutes before Alfred will be back."

"Marcus is telling everyone that he is my best friend. He showed up at the club," said Bron.

"What?"

"I need this like I need a hole in my head. My family and friends are livid and want to know what is going on, now," articulated Bron.

"He is trying to insert himself into our lives. Regardless of if we agree or not."

"Who are you talking about?" asked Pricilla.

We both turned our heads quickly.

"It concerns another situation."

"What situation?" asked Pricilla.

"None of your business," said Bron.

"Wow, the meeting is starting off super fun. Just think I had the nerve to come early," said Pricilla.

"Since when did you start coming to meetings early?" asked Bron.

"I am trying to impress everyone, and I was hoping to talk to Rot before the meeting started tonight. I was unable to *catch* her today, and I know that both you and Rot ended class early. I figured you all would be talking before the official meeting," said Pricilla.

"No, we were just killing time before the meeting."

"Yes, killing time," said Bron.

Pricilla started looking around the room and taking an inventory of everyone and their outfits. She had seen me earlier, but I assumed that she was making sure that I had not changed my outfit. She had on a different outfit. I guessed we were supposed to take it in.

"It sounds like a heated debate to me. Where is Rot?" asked Pricilla.

"And the gossip train is running smoothly," said Bron.

Suddenly, we heard someone shout, "Fire," and the alarm went off.

"What now? Is this official or is this a drill? Why would they hold a drill this late at night?"

"The scream did not sound like a drill," said Pricilla.

All the blood drained from Pricilla's face. I thought she was going to pass out. She yelled that she was once caught in a fire as a child because her family ignored the initial alarm. After a few moments, she screamed like a child and ran out of the room.

"I guess we cannot count on her in an emergency."

"Nothing new. Let's get out of here," said Bron.

"Where is Rot?"

"She is in the building. I hope she did not have any problems with her stalker. I keep telling her to get an escort."

"She is probably already at the front door," said Bron.

We started walking toward the stairs because you could not use the elevator. It was only three flights going down. You could hear a few people cursing and stumbling a bit. The lights went out. People started feverishly looking for their phone lights, so they would not fall. I was holding onto Bron and the banister. I just felt like something was happening, and it was not good.

The lights came back on. As I looked down the center of the stairs, I could see Alfred walking out the first-floor door. He had made it, but we had one more flight to go. We finally made it. Familiar and unfamiliar faces were in the lobby area when we heard another scream.

"There is no pulse. The person is dead in the stacks," said the student patron.

"Oh, my gosh."

I looked at Bron. This could not be Rot's death day. She pissed people off daily. It could not be her, but where was she? We walked faster to the crowd, and we both moved people to reach the body, but before we could fully reach the body, Bron asked the question that I did not want to ask out loud.

"Is it a woman?" asked Bron.

"No, it is not me. It is Dr. Pimpleton. Worried?" said Rot with the biggest smile on her face toward Bron.

I never hugged her so hard in my life, so I whispered in her ear, "Please never frighten us again like that."

"What is the fun in that?" asked Rot, matching my tone.

Lieutenant Alenzo and President Miller was telling the crowd to keep moving because there was an actual fire. Why was President Miller in the building? I informed her about the meeting, but I did not invite her.

The local police department and fire department were on site, so the situation was running as smoothly as possible. Since we were in the building with a dead body, we had to be escorted over to another location to give our statements. To my surprise, Malcolm, Mrs. Everstone, and Ms. Walker was standing in the mix.

Chapter Fifteen
Dr. Joanna Taylor

A LITTLE OVER ONE YEAR LATER…

The grant team is doing well for us. Alfred is working on his behavior and making improvements every day. Pricilla even helps him with his outfits at least once a week. She just buys them for him. She told me that he cannot hang with us looking like a moment in history. She can afford it now. Her new book is doing fabulously on the market, and Rot made sure that we are ready if her secret ever comes out. You do know her secret, right?

I just got tenure, and they fired my chair for discriminatory behavior. I received an undisclosed amount from the university. Rot and I have been documenting his behavior for a bit. We just had to wait for him to cross a line that he could not return from. Needless to say, my husband does not have to work anymore. Rot found me an attorney that specialized in that area.

Bron is doing great, especially today. He was just named the chair of the Criminal Justice Department. Rot helped Mrs. Everstone navigate university policy and her connections to ensure that Bron was exonerated of everything. Mrs. Everstone hired her. She was sick of the situation between the two of them. Rot found a problem with

Marie's statement and the *real* reason for the complaint, but that is another story for another time.

Rot has had huge success with her books and numerous publications from the grant. She stepped down from being chair because she is now only going to teach two classes per year (one each term) and offer a law clinic at the university connected to her law firm. "Free" educational labor from students. She labeled it a boutique firm. It may be small, but she makes a lot of money that triples her associate paycheck. One of the partners from her old law firm is her semi-partner. He brought with him many clients. She has a bigger share, and her name is first on the door. He obviously has a thing for her also, but that's another story. She says that I have problems with men. Hello, pot. Her first local case that spurred her to open her own office was defending Jonathan. He was charged with murdering Dr. Pimpleton.

We all *knew* that Jonathan did not do it. So, of course, we rallied around him with all our resources to save him. We found out that Jonathan was the hooded man at the protest and was feeding Ms. Walker and Marie information. This aspect never entered the courtroom. He was trying to impress Rot. He thought she wanted to help them but was not able to due to the university policy. Rot had a feeling that something was amiss, but she and Bron were also arguing about his path. Unbeknownst to me, they had a huge blowup before everything really started with Title IX. They both kept this from me.

It did not help Jonathan's case when the police found a shrine dedicated to Rot. The shrine also included comments stating that he planned to kill Marcus because he was disrespectful to Rot. Law enforcement did an illegal search, so none of this information entered the courtroom, and Jonathan walked out a free man. You would think that his father would have been happy about this aspect, but he looked mad on that day. We celebrated! Jonathan works at Rot's law firm now.

She has no fear of him doing anything to her, but that is another story, which I assume you would want more details about. It may have to do with the cameras in her office. We argue in the team grant meetings always, but what is new? Rot wants to produce more, and Bron does not want to run the statistics. Pricilla and Alfred help me smooth out the edges. The collective has gotten a little bigger, but we ensure that no one touches it. I guess you are also wondering what Marcus noticed in the picture. It looks like for now it still will be hidden, but we are scheduled to go up to school for alumni weekend. Hope to see you there...

CPSIA information can be obtained
at www.ICGtesting.com
Printed in the USA
BVHW060520091122
651495BV00003B/27